Here are nine stories of other worlds, other places, other times ... stories of truth and fiction and not so impossible dreams ... stories like –

Made to be Broken by E. C. Tubb

'Take me to your leader.' – Familiar words but when it comes to the real thing, they're only the start of the problem ...

The Eternal Theme of Exile: Three Enigmas II by Brian Aldiss

Three Enigmas – glittering dominoes masking the faces of experience and exile and the agony of eternal farewell ...

Sporting on Apteryx by Charles Partington

An analogue of reality we ignore at our peril ...

Accolade by Charles Grey

A new planet but a strange sort of Utopia ...

The Seed of Evil by Barrington J. Bailey

Personal obsession may triumph over insuperable obstacles – but there lies the catch ...

In the same series edited by John Carnell:

NEW WRITINGS IN SF 1–21

and edited by Kenneth Bulmer:

NEW WRITINGS IN SF 22–23

and published by Corgi Books

New Writings in SF – 23

edited by

Kenneth Bulmer

CORGI BOOKS
A DIVISION OF TRANSWORLD PUBLISHERS LTD

In 1964 John Carnell, in collaboration with Corgi Books founded the series NEW WRITINGS IN SF.
He edited volumes 1 to 21 until his death in 1972.

NEW WRITINGS IN SF–23
A CORGI BOOK 0 552 09681 4
Originally published in Great Britain
by Sidgwick and Jackson Ltd.

PRINTING HISTORY
Sidgwick and Jackson edition published 1973
Corgi edition published 1975

This book is set in Pilgrim 10/11 pt.

Corgi Books are published by Transworld Publishers Ltd.,
Cavendish House, 57–59 Uxbridge Road, Ealing,
London, W5 5SA

Made and printed in Great Britain by
Richard Clay (The Chaucer Press), Ltd., Bungay, Suffolk.

NOTE: The Australian price appearing on the back cover is the recommended retail price.

To

Commander Gene Cernan

Command Module Pilot Ron Evans

Lunar Module Pilot Jack Schmitt

for the Apollo 17 Moon Landing

who, in December of 1972, were not

THE LAST MEN IN THE MOON

CONTENTS

page

Foreword *by Kenneth Bulmer* 7

The Lake of Tuonela *by Keith Roberts* 11

Wagtail in the Morning *by Grahame Leman* 41

Made to be Broken *by E. C. Tubb* 57

The Eternal Theme of Exile: Three Enigmas II *by Brian W. Aldiss* 81

The Five Doors *by Michael Stall* 91

Sporting on Apteryx *by Charles Partington* 109

Rainbow *by David S. Garnett* 121

Accolade *by Charles Grey* 145

The Seed of Evil *by Barrington J. Bayley* 155

FOREWORD

by

KENNETH BULMER

THE response to the continuation of *New Writings* has been immediate and enthusiastic. There is a keen demand for the forward-looking, speculative, exciting and mind-provoking science fiction story as presented in this series. This volume contains nine stories dealing with a variety of themes and, in casting forward into the future, sf must inevitably highlight the dilemmas of today.

The problems of big city complexes are rapidly becoming perilously close to clichés in the non-sf media. The problems, their solutions and the fresh problems created by those solutions, are treated as almost-inescapable, as modern Erinyes—the so-called Furies. One major problem of cities is traffic with its attendant noise, dirt, pollution, smell, vibration and ever-present threat of accident and death. Fear of traffic is a deep psychological wound inflicted on us as soon as we learn to walk.

The other day on my way to a Board meeting of the Science Fiction Foundation I took the opportunity of walking through an old-fashioned high street that had been declared a pedestrian precinct. The place was cluttered, yet there was plenty of space for walking; the street was crammed with little shops with colourful window displays; borough market stalls provided opportunities for bargains; the air smelt clean; one or two supermarkets offered mass-production opportunities; the whole street delighted. I felt relaxed—and the shoppers did not to my eyes seem obsessed with that hurry hurry one associates with housekeeping shopping.

Back on the main road I was immediately and distastefully reminded of traffic as buses pounded past, cars and lorries hissed and vomited, motor cycles machine-gunned and fumes filled the air. The plunge towards zero on the gracious living chart was inescapable and edifying.

Science fiction has consistently advocated the use of all manner of pedestrian facilities in its use of pedways, rollerways, flyovers; and yet in the era of the forty-ton truck and articulated trailer we are told that overhead pedestrian walks are out of fashion. The farcical attempts at reaching agreement on a plan to do-over Piccadilly Circus indicate this, or so we are told. Traffic is a killer. For the transit of goods from point to point in the country a system already existing, and needing puny amounts of money to modernise to reduce road loads, is the network of canals.

Yet as a motorist and a user of canals for recreation I can see the other side of the coin. A car is essential to me, and I have spent many happy hours—and excruciating moments—on the narrow canals. The commercial canals can get those essential but awful trucks off much of the overloaded road system in conjunction with the railways—but how to transport goods to the warehouse door of the supermarket and the high street shop?

This is where another extravagant conception of the past can be called back into use. How would it be if you could lift your forty tons without expending energy, transport them at eighty miles an hour on relatively low-powered engines and drop them neatly down at the warehouse doorstep? As our American cousins would say—how does that grab you?

The answer is, of course, that it sounds too good to be true. Although this is essentially a science fictional idea at the present time, it is being actively worked on by at least two practical concerns, and is a part of the forward-thinking policy of the Airship Association.

The Airship Association has been formed to make people aware that the airship is the transport vehicle of the future. The membership list of the association contains the names of distinguished people: practical people, designers, scientists and artists, members of parliament, lords of the realm, journalists and flyers—people who know that the airship can solve many of the complex problems pressing in on us. Much more of the Airship Association will be heard in the future.

Therefore, when I first read the Keith Roberts' story that now leads off this volume of *New Writings*, I was immediately struck by the way in which the author, through the medium of sf, is able to parallel more than one of our twentieth-century problems while treating of an alien planet and canal system that is an analogue of our own. There is something about the peace and tranquillity of a canal that means a very great deal in the hurly burly of current life, and here Keith Roberts achieves a fine poetic intensity that says much of the way humanity is going.

The examination of dystopias is a task laid upon sf and here Grahame Leman does not shrink from opening blinkered eyes and of questioning the programming of unpredictable liveware. In volume 22 of *New Writings* Donald A. Wollheim in 'The Rules of the Game' indicated how the owner of the game can change the rules; here E. C. Tubb points out how a man faced with a soft science problem can similarly deal with the problem in non-superhuman terms.

Making his first appearance in these pages Charles Partington brings us face to face with the interlocking passions of love and hate set against an intriguing and tantalising background. Both Charles Grey and David Garnett make us look at the way men and women behave when faced with problems for which there appears no solution. In Barrington Bayley's long story one is conscious of the extent of time and of the impermanence of mankind's mark upon it, and in a deceptively simple way the author allows us to look into powers over and above those we take for granted, and which obsess so much of our current thinking. Michael Stall presents us with a hard-line depiction of a confrontation with forces of space in which the unravelment of the puzzle depends on sharpness of wit defeating fear. This is one for the aficionado.

New Writings in S-F is again fortunate in being able to present three more enigmas from Brian W. Aldiss and the penetration and brilliance of these contes continue. Brian Aldiss has been deeply involved in the back-breaking task of research, compilation and writing of an important new book about sf, *The Billion Year Spree*. This book, while undoubtedly being permeated by Brian Aldiss's own personal and strongly acute views, will unquestioningly be of great value in the further understanding and evaluation of sf.

The theme linking many of these stories, which must of brutal necessity appeal to any thinking and sensitive inhabitants of our planet, is a preoccupation with the witting and unwitting destruction of the environment and of life going on all about us.

Science has given foolish and greedy men the opportunity of raising up the Erinyes—the Furies—against the world; is it too fanciful a notion to suggest that sf has taken on the role of Apollo, to plead the cause of men and women? With a new toughened core of understanding of all the vision—so much fallen into disrepute of late—of the founding fathers of sf, perhaps the notion is not too fanciful, after all.

Horsmonden, KENNETH BULMER
January, 1973

THE LAKE OF TUONELA

by

KEITH ROBERTS

Filled with sensuous detail and the strange dream-like quality of far-off places, this evocation of an alien planet gains a memorable stature from the haunting awareness of place and people, of shining water and the sliding dappled banks of canals under an alien sun. Keith Roberts turns the art of sf to a delicate appraisal of moods and inclinations and yearnings in which humanity's own Bar-Ko *drives on with relentless terrestrial force. Locking-up to Hy Antiel, the canal was like a road to the Summit—a road paved with good intentions . . .*

THE LAKE OF TUONELA

THE dawn had been overcast; but by midmorning the weather had cleared. The small yellow sun of Xerxes burned in the planet's blue-green sky, waking shimmers and sparks from the little bow-wave the long boat drove ahead of it. The banks of the canal, lower here, were clothed with bushes and some stouter trees. Mathis, leaning his forearms on sun-warmed wood, felt the shadows stroke his cheek, touches of light and heat combined.

Here, in the bows of the vessel, the thud of her big single-cylinder engine was muted. He glanced back along the tented cargo space, turned once more to lean over the craft's side. The water was milky green; and some trick of light lent greater depth and perspective to the reflections than to the vegetation above. The tree leaves, small rounded sprays backlit to gold, passed smooth and silent fifty feet beneath the hull.

He studied the bow-wave, the fluctuating patterns within its stable form. The main crest curved from an inch or two before the vessel's blunt stem. Behind it the concave slope of water was glassy and clear. Some six inches ahead a smaller ripple began; the ends of this wavered, flickering forward and back in some pattern that seemed at the same time random and predetermined. Into it flowed the detailed images of branches; behind it the blue and gold melted into streaks that vanished in the deep green shadow of the hull.

He moved his shoulders, feeling the aches from the day before in back and arms. Thirty locks, in three flights of ten, had taxed his strength to the limit. The gates, unused for years, were grass-grown, nearly too stiff to move; also leaks had started, round the heel plates and worn paddle gear. Chamber after chamber refused to fill; it had taken the weight of the boat, butting at the timbers, to force the gates back. Locking down, the problem would be aggravated; but he had no intention of turning back.

He glanced at the chronometer strapped to his wrist, stared ahead again. For two days the canal had paralleled the course of GEM tracks, raw swaths of earth curving through the scrub and marshland that comprised much of Xerxes' Northern Continent; but the last of these had long since swung away. There were no signs of civilisation, either Terrestrial or Kalti, and no sounds save the sporadic piping of birds. The boat moved through a silence that the thudding of the engine only seemed to make the more complete.

He wondered, with something approaching interest, whether his absence had yet been noticed. A week had passed since leaving the lagoon that fringed Bran Gildo on the seaward side, climbing the vast lock flight that leads inland from the city. Mathis shrugged. If an alarm had been raised, it mattered little enough. Hidden for most of the time beneath the lapping tangle of branches, the boat would be invisible from a flyer; while the canals of the Southern Complex forked and meandered endlessly, joined by watercourse after watercourse, some natural, others artificial. The hamlets they had served, the mills and tiny manufactories, lay deserted now, the scrub growing up to and lapping across their walls; once lost in that complex, a spotter craft might search for a week and be no wiser at the end.

The air was humid beneath the trees. He wiped at his face and arms. On Earth, flies and midges would have made life burdensome; but the few flying insects of Xerxes, jewel-like creatures resembling terrestrial dragonflies, had no interest in blood. He watched one now, darting and hovering beneath the miniature moss-grown cliff of the bank. The thing swooped, took something from the surface of the water, vanished with a bright blur of wings. The water, he noted, still flowed steadily. The current came via bypass sluices from the high Summit Level ahead. It was an encouraging sign.

In front of the boat a purple-flowered shrub hung low across the water. Her cabin passed beneath its branches with a scrape and rustle. A dozen times already she had been forced to a halt, while Mathis and his steersman used machetes to hack a way through the half-choked water-course; but in the main the navigability of the canal after so many years disuse was a monument to the half-legendary Bar-Ab and his engineers.

Four Earth centuries ago, so ran the stories, Bar-Ab had been Prince of Bran Gildo, the palm-fringed city by the Salt Lagoon. He it was who in war after war had swept away the barbarous tribes of the interior, driving their remnants into reserves or into the sea; he also who had given to Xerxes the vast network of canals that till Terran Contact had remained the planet's major transportation system. From his line the Kalti, the Boatmen of Xerxes, claimed descent; when they troubled to claim anything at all. From the first, Mathis had been intrigued by them; the little dumpy men and the little dumpy women with their wide-brimmed, round-crowned hats and suits of Sunday black. Though the Kalti were a fast-vanishing race themselves. In every direction, through the swamps, across the uplands with their mile on mile of spindly forest, ran the broad trackways of the Ground Effect Machines; their windy rushing was the night-sound of Xerxes now, replacing the churring of frogs and hunting birds.

Mathis shrugged, and lit a cigarette. From the hundred or so he had brought with him, he allowed himself just two a day. He smoked carefully and slowly, thinking back to his interview with Jefferson, the Bran Gildo Controller. Just ten days ago, now.

He'd pushed his request as far as a Behaviourist (Grade 2A) reasonably could; and been mildly surprised at the result. A small but important circus had assembled to consider the proposition; Ramsden, head of Biology; an Engineer/Controller from the survey section; and Figgins from Liaison, complete with Earth-style secretary. It had been

Figgins who opened the attack; Figgins fat, and Figgins bearded.

'John, I feel I must make one point at the outset. This sort of thing is hardly your Department's concern.'

The Terran Complex, an air-conditioned cube of dural and glass, overlooked the brick-red ruins of the Old Palace; the place where Bar-Ab once sat, planning the network of waterways that would span a continent. A boat was passing, on the broad green moat that fronted the ruins, gliding above its mirror-image like a swan. A gay-striped awning covered it; on the foredeck lay a bare brown girl. Mathis shrugged. Difficult to keep his attention on the matter in hand. He said slowly, 'I never claimed my Department was involved. It's a personal project; and I've got a slab of leave come due.'

Figgins' secretary crossed her legs, looking bored. Ramsden, a neat, bald, compact man, ran his finger across an ornamental carafe—Kalti work—and frowned. The engineer doodled on a scratchpad. A little wait, while the Controller decided not to speak; and Figgins carried on.

'Speaking off the record,' he said, 'what would your object be in making a trip like this? What would you hope to prove?'

Mathis said, 'It's all in the report.'

Another wait. Nobody helped him.

The boat was nearly out of sight. He turned back from the window, unwillingly. The words sounded dry; meaningless with repetition. He said, 'We've been on Xerxes about one Earth generation. When we arrived we found a flourishing native culture. Backward on the sciences maybe but well up in the arts. We found a sub-culture, the Boatmen. They had a pictographic writing system like nothing we'd ever seen, and a religion we still haven't properly understood. One generation, and that culture is dying. I don't think we have that sort of privilege.'

Jefferson laid down the stylus he had been fingering. The click of metal on the rainbow-wood desk served to focus attention. Obscurely, Mathis wanted to smile.

The Controller said, 'I think we're rather wandering from the point. There are a lot of side effects to culture-shock that none of us much like. But they're inevitable given the situation in which we find ourselves.'

He glanced at Mathis, eyes bright blue beneath shaggy brows. It was a standard mannerism; a look calculated to convey old-world kindliness combined with shrewdness. 'We might not have learned as much as we ought from three hundred planets,' he said, 'but this much we do know. The day we made contact with Xerxes, existing social patterns were doomed. Mr. Mathis, you mentioned privilege just now. Let's all be logical.' He turned briefly to the big coloured map that covered most of one wall. 'The hinterland of the Northern Continent is largely swamp,' he said. 'In time, that swamp will be drained and reclaimed. Better standards of living are going to bring a higher birthrate, more mouths to feed. We shall need that land. As of this moment ... One Ground Effect Machine will traverse between Bran Gildo and Hy Antiel by any of half a dozen routes in a little under one day Planetary. It'll carry the payload of between five and six Kalti longboats, each of which would take a month on the trip. As I see it, our job isn't to resist a change that's already an accomplished fact. We're here to channel that change, help native cultures through a time of transition as smoothly and quickly as possible. In time, the Boatmen will learn new skills. Re-adapt. That's the way it has to be.'

Mathis said, 'In time, the Boatmen will cease to exist.'

The Controller nodded gravely. He said, 'That's also a possibility we must allow for.' He leafed through the docket on his desk. He said, 'You're asking for permission to take a Kalti boat through the Southern Complex by way of Hy Antiel Summit. And you still haven't answered Mr. Figgins' question. What's your ultimate object?'

Mathis said, 'The word goes that that complex is no longer navigable. That isn't true; and I'm going to prove it. A tenth of what we spent last year on GEM terminals would restore it to full working use. And a hundredth of the labour. I want to see that happen; and I also want the matter of the Kalti culture raised at the next sitting of the Extraterrestrial Council. With your permission, I'm applying for a personal hearing. I want the Boatmen protected, and the entire Northern Continent declared a Planetary Reserve.'

The Controller raised his brows slightly. He said, 'Well, that's your privilege. Ramsden, what do you feel about all this?'

The biologist rubbed his chin. 'There's another factor of course,' he said in his quiet, precise voice. 'Preservation equals stagnation; stagnation equals deterioration. This sort of thing has been tried enough before. In my experience, it's never worked.'

Figgins grunted. 'It seems to me,' he said, 'that you're starting from unsound premises anyway. These people, the Kalti; I haven't seen many of 'em clamouring for help. Could be they don't want the old way any more than we do. You preservationists are all alike, John. None of you can take the broad view.'

Mathis shook his head, still vaguely amused. How explain? If Figgins didn't understand, it was because he didn't want to. Study a Kalti pictograph, the swirls that were tenses, the shadings that were words, and the answer was plain enough. Through every design, like a great hyphen, slashed the *Bar-Ko*, the mark of the One who made water and earth, the green leaves and the sky. At the start of time, He decreed all things to be. If a man was to die, or a culture fail, then these facts were preordained; true a milion years ago, and true for ever. This was all you needed; know it, and you knew the Boatmen.

But the Controller was speaking again. This time to the engineer.

'Mr. Sito, do you have anything to add?'

Sito shrugged. 'I'd say the whole thing was a pipedream. That cut hasn't been used in thirty years; even the Boatmen don't seem to know much about it any more. I shouldn't think you'd get through to Summit Level; and if you did, do you know the length of that tunnel?'

Mathis said, 'Not precisely, no.'

The other made a face. 'That's my point. Those blighters dug like beavers. There's a tunnel up in the Northern Marshes, Kel Santo, that measures out at ten kilometres. We've had to put scaffolding through nearly a kilometre to hold the roof; and Kel Santo's never been out of maintenance. Take a boat into Hy Antiel and jam, and you'd not walk back out. It isn't a chance I'd take.'

The Controller nodded. 'Yes, Mr. Ramsden?'

The biologist said carefully, 'I have to point out it's not too healthy an area. Most of our cases of Xerxian fever have been brought in from the Antiel range. It's spread by a free-swimming amoeboid, gets into the smallest abrasion. Leave that untreated, and you're in trouble. I've seen some native cases; the medics call it the Shambles.'

The Controller said briskly, 'Right, I think that gives us all we need.' The stylus tapped the table-top again, with finality. 'I'm not unsympathetic,' he said to Mathis. 'Far from it. As far as appeals go, I'll forward your case with pleasure; we all know every frontiersman has that right. But for the rest; I have to think, first and foremost, of the safety of Base personnel. Both your own and the party we'd have to send out if you went missing. So . . . request refused. I'm sorry.' He shuffled the papers together, handed them across the desk and rose.

Ramsden caught up with Mathis in the outer office. By mutual consent, they took the elevator to the ground floor bar. Earth interests on Xerxes were expanding steadily; they were brewing something on the planet now that tasted remarkably like whisky. The biologist called for doubles, drank, put the glass down and puffed a pipe alight. He said, 'Hm, sorry about that. Hardly expected anything else though. Disappointed?'

Mathis smiled. He said slowly, 'Not particularly.'

The other glanced up sharply; and it occurred to Mathis

that alone of the committee, Nathan Ramsden had understood his real purpose. Better, perhaps, than he understood it himself. He'd known the biologist a long time. Once, a thousand years back on another planet, he'd been in trouble. He rang Ramsden; and Ramsden had listened till the bursting words were done. Then he said quietly, 'I see. Now, what's the first thing I can do to help?'

The older man took another sip of the pseudo-Scotch. He said, 'As you know, it's not my custom to offer unwanted advice. But I'm offering some now. Go home.'

Mathis stayed silent. He was seeing the canals; the endless shadings of green and gold, puttering of the long black hulls, interlacing of leaf and branch shadows in the brown-green mirror of the water. By pictograph, an answer might be made. The white and blue swirls formed themselves unasked, inside his head.

Ramsden set the glass down. He said, 'This'll be my last tour anyway. I'm looking forward to putting my feet up on an Honorary Chair somewhere. You're still young, John; you've got a year or two left yet.'

Mathis said vaguely, 'I suppose we're as young as we feel.'

The biologist said, 'Hmm ...' He waited a moment longer; then rose. He said, 'Drink up. I've got an hour before my duty tour; I've got someone I'd like you to meet.'

The steersman called behind him; a high, sharp sound, like a yap. The Kalti waved and grinned, pointing to the bank; and Mathis smiled, nodding in return. Ahead rose a line of hills, outliers of the Hy Antiel massif. An arm of forest swept down to the canal; it enclosed a grassy clearing, quiet and golden with sunlight. The Boatman swung the painted shaft of the stern oar, nosing the big craft in towards the bank.

In the Lagoon, close under the old white city walls, the long vessels lay tied each to each; the sun winked from brass-strapped chimneys and round portglasses, gleamed on the painted coamings of cabins. On each stempost, knotted ropework was pipeclayed to whiteness; above each roof were the big running lamps with their filigree-work of brass; on each side, somewhere, was the mark of the God, the *Bar-Ko* with its sprays of leaves, gold and white and blue. Ramsden strolled beside the bright herd of boats, wiping his face and neck with a bandanna. He paused finally beside a craft tied up some distance from the rest, and called. 'Can't get my tongue round these Kalti names,' he said. 'I just call him Jack.'

The Boatman who bobbed from the diminutive bow cabin was slimmer than most of his people. His bland face with the dark, slightly tilted eyes looked very young; to Mathis, he seemed little more than a boy. He grinned, ducking his head, showing a half-moon of brilliant teeth. Ramsden said, '*Hoki*, Jack. *Hoki, a-aie?*' The Kalti grinned again and nodded, waving a slender hand. The biologist stepped across to the raised prow, dropped, grunting, to the foredeck. Mathis followed him.

Hoki, the coffee-like beverage brewed by the Boatmen, had not at first been to Mathis' taste; but he had grown accustomed to its sharp, slightly bitter flavour. He squatted in the cramped cabin, the thin-shelled, brightly painted cup in his fingers, waited while Ramsden mopped his face again. 'He speaks a bit of Terran,' he said. 'Not much, but I think you'll get by. His parents are dead. He's twenty-five; usually their marriage contracts are settled before they're out of their teens but Jack's still working single-handed. Bit of an oddball, in many respects.'

The Boatman grinned again. He said, 'Too right,' in a clipped, slightly sing-song voice. He took Mathis' cup, poured more of the brownish fluid. The pot in which it was brewed, like all Kalti artifacts, was gaily decorated; the little discs of copper hanging round its circumference tinkled as he set it down.

Mathis looked round the cabin. It wasn't usual for Terrans to be invited aboard a Kalti boat. Nests of drawers and cupboards lined the walls. No inch of the tiny living space seemed wasted; there were earthenware bowls, copper measures and a dipper, a barrel for water storage, a minute stove. He wondered vaguely how Ramsden had come to know the Boatman. He seemed well enough at home.

The biologist lit his pipe again, staring through the open doors at the sparkling expanse of the lagoon. 'This man will take you to Hy Antiel,' he said quietly. 'By the old route, through the Antiel Range. He's a bit of a patriot in his own way too, is young Jack.'

Mathis narrowed his eyes. He said, 'Why're you doing this, Nathan?'

The older man shrugged and raised his brows. 'Because,' he said, 'if you intend to go, and I feel you do, I'd rather you have a good man with you. That way you stand a chance of coming back.' He prodded at the pipe bowl with a spent match. 'Just one thing,' he said. 'If they drag you out by the back hair, as they probably will, I shan't know a thing about it. I've got troubles of my own already . . .'

He had one final memory; of sitting on the cabin roof of the great boat later that day, watching a vessel come in from planetary west. Through the glasses she seemed to make no progression, hanging shadowlike against the glowing shield of water. The figures that crowded her rocked, as she rocked, slowly from side to side. From them drifted a thread of sound; a single note, harsh and unnatural, taken up and sustained by voice after voice.

Mathis touched the young Kalti on the shoulder, pointed. 'Jack,' he said, 'what's that?'

'*Kaput,*' said the Boatman unexpectedly. 'All finish.'

Mathis said musingly, 'All the decks were dense with stately forms . . .' He glanced down sharply. He said, 'You mean it's a funeral?'

'All finish,' said Jack. 'Yes. Bloody bad luck.'

The canal shallowed towards the edges, banked with fine silt. He heard the slither and bump as the flat-bottomed craft grounded, and shrugged. A few minutes' work with the poles would shift her, at first light. For safety's sake he still carried a line ashore. The ground, unexpectedly soft, wouldn't hold a mooring spike. He tethered the boat instead to a sapling at the water's edge. He sat a while watching the shadows lengthen, the gold fade from the little space of grass. From the cabin at his back came shufflings, once a tinkle as the Kalti worked, preparing the mess of beans on which the Boatmen habitually lived. With the dusk a little breeze rose, blowing from the hills, heavy with the scent of some night flower.

The Kalti bobbed from the cabin slide. 'All done,' he said. 'Too quick.'

Mathis turned, stared up at the high line of hills losing themselves in the night. 'Jack,' he said, 'are we going to make it?'

The Boatman nodded vigorously. 'One time,' he said. 'No sweat. Too bloody quick.'

He had conned De Witt at Base into knocking him up a generator and headlamp to supplement the lighting of the Kalti boat. It rested now on the forward cabin top, an untidy arrangement of batteries and wires. He ran a hand across the motor casings as he smoked his final cigarette. The canal was restless; cheepings sounded and close plops, once a heavier crashing of branches followed by the *swack-swack-swack* of a bird taking off from water. The banks, and the shaggy bushes lining them, were mounded velvet; between them the water gleamed, depthless and pale. It seemed the canal itself gave off a scent; chill and pervasive. The moon of Xerxes was rising as he sought his sleeping bag.

The morning was difficult. The channel, much overgrown here, had silted badly; time and again the boat grounded, sliding to a halt. The pole tip sank in the softness, raising blackish swirls that stained the clear green. The Kalti, patient and expressionless, worked engine and steering oar, using the boat's power now to drive her forward, now to draw back from an impassable shoal. The sun woke shimmers from the thread of water remaining, while Mathis sweated and heaved. By midday, he guessed they had covered little more than a mile. They rested a while, drawn beneath a tangle of bushes; and he heard the echoing whistle of a flyer, somewhere to the north. He waited, frowning. For a time the machine seemed to circle, the sound of its motors eddying on the wind. Then the noise faded. It did not return.

By mid-afternoon the condition of the waterway had improved. The boat resumed its steady pace, gliding still between high mounded bushes. Some of the branches bore viciously sharp thorns; Mathis, standing in the bow, swung a machete, lopping a path clear for the steersman. That night he was glad of his rest.

Next morning they reached the foot of a long lock flight that climbed steadily into the hills. The chambers were well spaced, the pounds between them a mile or more in length. Over each pair of gates the *Bar-Ko* rusted in its bright iron frame, a valediction from the long-dead Prince. Viridian creepers had wound themselves into and through the scrollwork of the supports; their long tendrils brushed Mathis' face as the boat glided beneath. On the following day they entered the first of the cuttings.

For some time the ground to either side had been trending steadily upward; now the canal sides, still heightening, closed together, becoming near-vertical cliffs of dark purple rock. The strata of which they were composed were seamed and cracked; between the layers massive trees somehow found lodgement. The root bosses, gnarled and lichened, glistened with water that oozed its way steadily through the stone. Above, the higher trunks were festooned with the brilliant creeper. Some inclined at precarious angles, meshing their branches with those of their fellows on the opposite bank. From them the tendrils swayed, dropping masses of foliage to the water fifty or sixty feet beneath. Later the cutting, still immensely deep, opened out; here lianas, as thick as or thicker than Mathis' arms, stretched pale and taut from the leaf canopy to the shelving rock. They did not, he saw, descend vertically but inclined on both sides at a slight angle to the water; so that driving between them was like passing through the forest-ribs of an enormous keel.

The cutting had one advantage; the height and density of the trees had thinned out secondary growth. The water still ran clear and green; the rock, though friable, seemed not to discolour it. Mathis sat in the damp warmth, hearing the magnified beat of the engine echo back from the high cliff to either side. In time he grew tired of staring up; then it seemed his sense of scale was altered. The bank beside which the boat slid, the foot or so of rock at the water's edge, became in itself a precipice, sheer and beetling. The sheet of lichen, the tiny mosslike plants clinging to the stone, were meadows and trees, above which the menacing shapes drifted like clouds. The tips of the great falls of creeper, touching the boat, discharged showers of drops that fell like storms of icy rain.

He thought vaguely of Ramsden, back at Base; the delight the biologist would take in the strange plant forms surrounding him. With the thought came another, less surely formed; a sense of loss, an aching regret at the necessity for actions. He knew himself better now; and understood more fully the nature of his journey. The notion, once admitted, remained with him, his mind returning to it with the insistence with which the tongue-tip probes the wound of an extraction. This seemed to be the truth; that because nothing, no homecoming, waited beyond the hill range he was drawn forward, because of desolation and emptiness he had to go on. The trees stretched their ranks over the edge of rock above him; beyond he knew lay others and still more, mile on endless mile of forest haunted by rodents and owls. There were empty hamlets, empty villages, empty towns maybe, lapped by the rising green, wetted by rains, warmed by summer suns. He experienced a curious desire, transient yet powerful, to know that land; but know it in detail, hollow by hollow, as he knew the lines of his palms. He wondered at the state of mind, not wholly new to him; and wondered too at a curious notion Ramsden had once expressed that the Loop, in scrambling a man, never reassembled the same being twice. The oddity was allied to another, better known; that over seven years or so the elements of the body, the pints of water and pennorths of salt, are wholly changed so that physically and intimately one becomes a different being. Yet the thinking part, whichever that might be, goes on for ever. Hurting, and giving pain.

A mile into the cutting the engine stalled, with a thud.

He was amused, momentarily, at the flash of panic aroused in him. The mind, it seems, insists on clinging to patterns once known; maybe to the point of death. The long hull was swinging and losing way, pushed by the faint current from ahead; he fended with the pole, felt the bottom bump gently against mud. He climbed to the catwalk above the cargo space, walked steadily astern.

Round the rear of the vessel, immediately above the propeller, ran a narrow ledge. The Kalti was squatting on it, gripping one-handed, groping with the other arm beneath the water. For the journey, he had affected Terran garb; a sleeveless woollen jerkin, printed with Fair Isle patterns and plentifully daubed with oil, and a pair of frayed and faded jeans. His harsh, longish hair hung forward; between jeans and pullover showed a half-moon of olive skin. He straightened when Mathis spoke, grinning his inevitable grin; Mathis wondered suddenly if it was no more than a reflex of the nerves. 'All stuck up,' he said. 'Jolly bad luck.'

Mathis climbed down beside him. The tip of a nobbled branch protruded from the water; below, its cloudy shape was visible for a foot or more before vanishing in the greenness. He tugged at it. It felt immovable. His reach was longer than the Kalti's; he felt carefully for the propeller boss, traced his finger back along the battered edge of the blade. The log was jammed firmly between propeller and hull.

The Kalti pulled the sweater over his head, balancing with care. He folded the garment neatly and slid into the water. Mathis followed, feeling the buoyant chill.

From this viewpoint, the black hull seemed immense. The

mud of the canal bottom sucked at his feet; he grabbed for breath, ducked, surfaced again. He ran fingers across the curving, crusted planks, carefully, remembering Ramsden's injunction. The Kalti heaved at the branch. It moved anti-clockwise an inch or so, jammed again. Half-rotten, the wood was difficult to grip. Mathis clung to the step, exploring again with his free hand. The edge of the big prop had bitten deeply into the waterlogged fibres. He shook his head, made washout motions with his palm above the water.

He paddled to where he could once more swing himself aboard. The ironwood grating at the stern lifted readily enough. Beneath it the shaft gleamed dully, secured to the primitive gearbox by a flexible jawed coupling. He fingered the heavy hand-forged bolts. The Kalti nodded, and grinned again.

De Witt had made up a toolkit for the boat. None of the set spanners fitted; he used an adjustable, working carefully so as not to burr the edges of the nuts. As he worked a light drizzle began, drifting in greyish veils from the heights above.

The nuts came clear, finally. He tapped the bolts back through the fibrous coupling plate, and gripped the shaft. It wouldn't budge.

He sorted the toolkit for the longest crowbar. A wooden wedge pressed against the gearbox end protected the coupling from damage. He leaned his weight carefully. The shaft stayed firm. He took a breath, jerked. The thing slid backward through the packing gland, with a faint creak. He reached behind him, pulled. The branch rolled clear and sank.

He eased the shaft forward, reconnected. He sat back, wiping his hands on a piece of fibrous husk. He said, 'Hoki, Jack?' The Kalti raised his thumbs. He said, 'Dear me, yes.' He scrambled forward, over the cargo space.

By mid-afternoon they were clear of the cutting. Beyond, the land fell away with startling speed to a steep and ragged valley. Across it strode an aqueduct, massive arches built of the same purplish rock. To one side, sluices discharged water from the canal lips with a sullen roar. The spray from the fall drifted back, obscuring the defile. Mathis, gripping the boat's rail, imagined the black hull, topped with the tilted brightwork of the cabins, sliding so high in the air. He saw the vessel from the viewpoint of an observer in the tangled valley bottom. Beyond the great structure the rock walls once more swooped together; and the Kalti moored for the night.

In the second cutting they were delayed again, this time by mud and weed. The weed, slimy strings of it twenty feet or more in length, wrapped itself persistently around the propeller, building a solid ball between blades and hull. As the obstructions formed the Boatman sliced them away patiently. Mathis poled dully, disinterested in time; later the machetes were once more brought into use. Finally the narrows were passed; the second cutting opened up ahead. The rock rose steeply, a hundred feet or more, clothed still for most of its height with living green. Through much of the day the far lip caught the sun; the feathery trees that lined it seemed to burn, haloed with pale gold. Later, clouds grew across the sky. The drizzle returned; and a thin mist, veiling the highest rock. In time the mist crept lower, rolling slowly, clinging in tongues to the water.

He was standing beside the steersman on the little stern grating. The Kalti grunted, pulling his lips back from his teeth. Mathis shook his head; and the Boatman waved an arm. '*Mutta-a*,' he said to the surrounding heights. '*Mutta-a. Kaput*.'

Mutta-a. Mutti, Maman ... The first sound of any mammal's voice will make. Mathis said, 'You mean it's haunted.' Perhaps this was why the Kalti were disinclined to talk.

'*Mutta-a*,' said Jack, nodding vigorously. 'Rather silly.'

Mathis said, 'I can believe it.'

He walked forward. The mist, or cloud-base, had thickened again; the tree-limbs, some bleached, pushed through it, with curious effect. He was interested to find it was still possible to feel unease. He savoured the sensation, with some care.

The huge walls angled to the left. The boat edged round the bend; and a black mouth showed ahead. The sloping hillside in which it was set climbed to unguessed height. Bushes clung to it; above hung the trunks of the endless forest. The opening itself was horseshoe-shaped, its throat densely black. From fifty yards, he smelled its breath; ancient and chill. Mathis rubbed his face; then swung to the cabin top to start the generator.

This was the Tunnel of Hy Antiel.

He turned the handlamp. The ribbon of water ahead was tarry, non-reflecting. To either side the close brick walls were festooned with red and green slime; larger masses, leprous-white in the light, hung from the half-seen roof. As the boat brushed at them they broke with soft snaps. From the brickwork of the tunnel fell a steady chill rain.

He listened, turning his head. What he had not been prepared for was the din. The thudding of the boat's diesel echoed massively from the curved walls; but there were other sounds. A sighing rose to something like a roar, fled forward and back along the shaft. Maybe the boat had scraped the side, some sprag touched her hull; God only knew. The brick throat threw echoes back on themselves, lapping and distorting. At first the sounds had troubled him; but they had been travelling two hours or more, he had grown accustomed to the place.

He pitched the light farther ahead. For some time now a deeper roar had been growing in intensity. He saw its source finally; a curtain of clear water, sparkling as it fell from the roof. At its base the surface boiled and rippled, throwing up wavering banks of brownish foam.

This was the fourth airshaft he had seen. He ducked, tortoise-fashion, into the little bow castle, heard the cannonade pass down the long tarpaulins of the cargo space to the stern. The big boat rocked; the sighing came again, mixed with the fading roar.

Here, in the encroaching dark, the swimming sense of motion was intensified. A memory returned to him, odd and unconnected; and he nearly smiled. It was of a journey back from London to his home, when he was a tiny child. On the trip down, the monorail whispered and clattered, flashing through tunnel after tunnel beneath the great complexes of buildings; but now the darkness pressed uniform and baffling against the rounded panes of the carriage. He had asked, finally, when this tunnel would end; and his father, momentarily surprised, had dropped a hand to his shoulder and laughed. 'It isn't a tunnel, John,' he said. 'It's the night...'

He leaned back, head against the bulky survival pack. He felt tired and a little dizzy. Maybe it was the fumes that hung in the shaft. He lit his daily cigarette, and closed his eyes. He saw with remarkable clarity the white walls and green palm-clumps of Bran Gildo, the unused watchtowers pushing their dunce-cap roofs into the turquoise sky. It seemed he could smell the hot, spiced air, the fragrance of spike-leaved shrubs where the Terran girls walked with their pleated kilts and strapped native sandals and long bronzed limbs. From beyond the Palace walls came the sounds of the city's traffic, cartbells mixed with the whine of the electric buggies that were a gift from an ever-benevolent Earth. He opened his lids, seeing the slime-hung walls. The two images, so disparate, were yet interlinked; pieces of an equation that one day must be solved.

He reached above him to the pack. Strapped to it was the holster of the standard ten-shot Walther issued under space regs to every serving frontiersman, beside it the bulkier grip of the Gyrojet pistol Ramsden had at the last insisted he carry. He shook his head. Perhaps he had studied the pictographs too long. The philosophy of weapons, alien to the Kalti, had become all but alien to him. The One beyond, whose Sign is the glimmering horizon, decreed all things to be; death and life came in their turn, and were acceptable. To oppose circumstance, to impose the will, had come to seem a heresy. It was not will that drove him, or the boat;

rather it was a sense of inevitability, of the fitness of his course to some purpose that continued to evade him. There was no sense of struggle; consequently there could be no achievement. The massive fetish of the guns reminded him of much that he had wished to leave behind. He had thought at first he might drop them over the side; but an ennui, the same listlessness that stilled his tongue at the meeting, came between intention and the act. There they lay; there let them be.

He must have slept; certainly he dozed, for when his eyes once more opened the engine of the boat was quiet. The cabin lamps were lit; Jack banged and clattered at the little stove.

He rose, awkward in the confined space. For a moment he was disoriented; and the child's confusion returned so that it seemed the boat must have passed the tunnel. Then he saw how the lamplight glowed in fans across wet brickwork; the air he drew into his lungs was chill and stale. He turned to the Boatman; and the Kalti grinned. 'Too far,' he said. 'Not much good.'

They were moored to what seemed to be the remains of a little wharf. Lines of rusting iron rings were let into the brickwork. He swung to the cabin top, started the generator. The lampbeam showed the black, unrippling water stretching ahead. To the right, joining the main line at a sharp angle, was a second shaft. The stonework of the curving groin where tunnels met looked new and fresh. He pointed to the shaft; but the Kalti shrugged, making washout motions with his hands. He said again, 'Not much good.'

With the boat motionless, the silence of the tunnel was complete. He lay a long time hearing the quietness hiss in his ears. Finally, sleep came; and with it, dreams. They were untenanted, yet precisely detailed. They concerned ancient buildings, places seen once on Earth. A gatehouse, lost in a wood of tall elms; a street of white-walled cottages; a flight of turf steps before a great stone Minster.

Finally it seemed he sat in an upper room of a very large

house. The room, a study, looked out on wings of crumbling stone. Beyond were formal gardens, arbours framing leaden nymphs and gods. In the dream he knew with certainty that he would never leave the room, never rise from the chair; and that the light, the afternoon light, would never change.

The Kalti roused him. He was giddy and lightheaded; and his eyes seemed gummy, as though he had not slept. He ate the bean stew the boy set before him with little interest. Afterwards he walked to where the jetty, if jetty it was, narrowed, the stone fairing into the smooth brick of the shaft. His purpose satisfied, he stepped back to untie the ropes from the heavy rings. The Kalti swung up the engine; he poled the bow from the wharf, and the journey was resumed.

Twice in the hours that followed echoing roars from ahead warned of fresh ventshafts. Each discharged its torrent of water into the canal; but staring up as the boat approached Mathis could detect no gleam of outside light. One shaft seemed partially choked; fibrous roots hung twisting in the downpour, their tips pale and rotted. At eleven hundred the boat passed a line of low flood arches. Water from the canal lip poured beneath them in steady greenish sheets. Mathis turned the lamp. At first it seemed a black void opened beyond; but this was a trick of light. The rock, covered with some dark, non-reflectant growth, was very close.

The workings in the tunnel were complex, like none he had seen. He wondered at their age. He asked the Kalti, shouting above the engine; but the Boatman shook his head. '*Mutta-a,*' he said. He spread his fingers, and again. Many generations.

The tunnel was very old.

To his other questions there was no reply. The tunnel was very long.

Later in the day the brickwork ended.

The effect was odd. Beyond the shaft sides, a jet half-circle seemed to form and widen. He watched the spreading band a moment, puzzled; then the tunnel was falling away behind. The engine noise, that for so long had pounded in his ears, faded as the stern of the boat drew clear.

He swung the big lamp left and right, discovering no sign of walls; the gloom ahead was likewise unrelieved. At last the abundance of summit water was explained; they had entered an underground lake, of unknown size. He wondered fleetingly if Bar-Ab and his engineers had known. Had they plotted the extent of the cavern, tunnelled to its brink; or had the miners burst into the void, startled and unsuspecting...

On impulse, he angled the light upward. Above, suspended it seemed from an infinite height, the *Bar-Ko*, dark red and dripping, marked the way. Beyond the great iron Sign hung another; and another, dimly seen.

He nodded to himself. They had known.

The tunnel had been loud with noise. Running through the void, the opposite effect seemed to hold true. Silence, like the dark, pressed in on the boat; almost it seemed the cavern deadened sound, so that twice he scrambled to the cabin roof convinced the engine was no longer running. Each time he was reassured by the thumping ninety feet astern. Once he tried sounding, with the longest pole, but could touch no bottom. He turned his wrist in the beam of De Witt's spotlight, holding the chronometer close up to his face. He was surprised to see an hour had elapsed since quitting the shaft.

With time, the absence of sensation affected him strongly. The tunnel sounds returned, the whisperings and long sighs; but they were in his ears. Also it seemed that lights appeared, far across the water. It was as if a fairy army drove to meet him, yet forever receded. He rubbed his face, knuckling at his eyes; and the lights were gone.

Finally a fresher breeze blew from ahead. Also he saw, above the endless line of markers, a fold of stone that was the dripping of the cavern roof. Ghostings of grey appeared to either side; then, suddenly, the cavern walls began to close back in. The slime-hung brickwork returned; and he stared behind him at the velvet dark. He said, 'The Lake of Tuonela.'

Tuonela, where dead spirits walk.

In the outer world, the time was thirteen hundred. The abstraction counted for little here. He wound the chronometer, staring up while the bow of the vessel bumped gently at what looked at first sight to be the gate of a stop lock. The journey was ended.

The tilted beam of light rolled slowly, illuminating a slope of wet, smooth rock. At its summit, the side of the second great caisson showed its panels of rusting iron. More iron, columns and tie rods, rose into the dark. Beyond was an engine house. The round-topped windows stared like dim sockets; above them the buttressed column that was the chimney grew up into the stone, thrusting for the open air. Mathis grinned, showing his teeth. He said softly, 'The crazy bastards.'

He sat on the cabin roof and lit a cigarette. He felt closer to Bar-Ab and his men than he would have thought possible. He rubbed the beard-stubble on his chin and asked himself, how could they have done it? How could they carve through twenty miles of rock, with pickaxes and plumb bobs, and keep their line and level? Those engineers in kilts and plumes? Like the Incas, their priests used the Rope of Thorns. Like the Victorians, they knew black powder and the barrow run. Like both, they vanished. They left . . . this.

They built an Inclined Plane, inside a bloody hill.

A sound at his elbow made him turn. The Kalti's face was a pale mark in the gloom. He waved an arm at the monstrousness; the caissons, the engine house, the rails with their great red bogies. 'Make go,' he said. 'Make go.'

Mathis threw the half-smoked butt into the water. Sito would have given his back teeth for this. 'Yes, Jack,' he said. 'We must make it go . . .'

There was coal; great bunkers of it, growing here and

there a rich skin of mould. Coal, but no kindling. For that they stripped the powdering frames from windows, boards from the engine-house floor. Fuel oil from the boat's depleted tank would fire the furnace. The boiler they filled painfully, a bucket at a time. The top caisson already held water; the gate of the lower for a time refused to close. Mathis rigged a fourfold purchase from a mooring bollard, strained the thick iron partially shut; the boat herself, thundering in reverse, completed the job. Brown foam boiled; the big door closed, with protesting squeals. They lit the furnace then, sat an hour while pressure built to working head. Round the boiler were heavy riveted straps. In time the rivet heads began to sizzle and steam.

There was a bank of gauges, each set in a plate of foliated brass. The markings on the faces made no sense. It was guesswork, all the way.

Mathis edged the regulator forward.. A rumbling; rust flew, in a thin rain. Below, the long chains stretched over the rock clanked to tautness. The boat slopped against the chamber side; the engine slowed as the ancient gearing felt the load. Steam roared from a union; and the boat was climbing, inching sideways up the Plane. The headlight, blazing, drew level with Mathis, began to pass. The Kalti heaved at the caisson side, adding his strength to the strength of the machine. He was happy. He had done what the strange Terri wanted; now others would come, with their engines that tore away rock and plucked down trees. And the long cuttings would once more fill. His head made pictures; he saw the blue and red stars that were the lamps of boats, sailing all night long from Bran Gildo to Hy Antiel.

A chain link parted, with a ringing crash. Mathis, sweating, wrenched at the emergency brake with blistered hands. The caisson, with its hundred thousand gallon load, lurched backward on the slope; and the Kalti's heels shot from under him.

'Oh dear,' said Jack. The bogies, gathering speed, severed his arm, ploughed crashing across his chest. The caisson took the water it had quitted with a thunderous splash. A tinkling; the headlight on the cabin roof swayed sideways, and was extinguished.

The tunnel portal was set into a low, mounded hill. Beyond it the canal was fringed with low shrubs that blazed with smoky orange blossom. Above, saplings hung graceful and still, their sprays of rounded leaves catching the sunset light.

To an observer stationed at the tunnel mouth, the twin lamps of the Kalti vessel would have appeared at first like dim brown stars. For some time, such are the curious optics of tunnels, the stars would have appeared to grow no closer; then, suddenly it seemed, they swam forward. Between them the outlines of the boat became visible; the knotted headropes of the prow, the tilted cabin with its ornamented ports. Behind, sliding into the light, came the long tented cargo space; the engine-house, hazed with blue; the stern deck with its grating, the *Bar-Ko* vaunting white and gold on the rounded black sides. The steersman, in once-white slacks and shirt, leaned wearily on the painted shaft of the oar. His face was fringed with a stubble of beard; from time to time he glanced down, frowning, at a bundle near his feet. In places the canvas of which it was composed was soaked and dark; and a runnel of fluid had escaped, staining the boat's dull side.

To Mathis, the transition from darkness to the light seemed curiously unreal. He smelled the sweetness of the grass, heard the wind rustle in the tops of trees and frowned again, shaking his head as if to clear it. His brain recorded, but sluggishly. Ahead and to the left, twin hills marked the position of Hy Antiel. This was the Summit Pound; five miles ahead the lock flight began that led to the city, stepping in green steps down a green and grassy hill. He'd walked beside it often enough, it seemed in some other life.

He squinted up, at the high dusting of gold. To the right showed the pilings of a mooring place. Little bushes surrounded it, throwing their branch-shadows across the water. He turned the oar, unused as yet to the boat's response, glided the long vessel to the bank.

He was uncertain of the forms to be employed. He chose a spot finally; a grassy knoll beneath the branches of a broad, spreading tree. He had brought a spade and mattock from the boat; he wiped his forehead, and began to dig. Later he drove a stake into the grass at the head of the fresh-turned mound. To it he lashed a crosspiece for the *Bar-Ko* sign; then there was nothing more to do.

He searched the Kalti's few possessions. He found a breechcloth of silk, a scarf, a broad-brimmed, round-crowned hat; and a bolero crusted with pearly buttons, the sort of garment a Boatman would wear on a feast-day in Bran Gildo. In a bag closed by a drawstring were two brooches set with semi-precious stones, a nugget of what looked to be iron pyrites and a lock-key charm in gold. There were also a prayer-roll sealed with the *Bar-Ko* mark, and a much-thumbed packet of postcards showing bare-breasted Terran girls. These last he returned to the bag before tucking it carefully away.

He didn't wish to eat. Instead he brewed up the Kalti coffee, drinking several cups. Slightly alcoholic, the drink had a heady effect. He smoked a cigarette, saw to his mooring stakes and spread his sleeping-bag on the cabin roof. The spinning in his head was worse; he closed his eyes, and was quickly asleep.

He woke some time before the Xerxian dawn. To planetary east, the first faint flush of green heralded the sun. The canal was a silver mirror, set between velvet trees; and Barbara watched him from the bank, her chin in her hand. The light gleamed palely from her hair.

He pushed himself up on one elbow, and smiled. 'Hello,' he said. 'Are you coming on board?'

She considered, smiling in her turn, before she slowly shook her head. 'No, thanks,' she said. 'I think once was enough. I don't think I could go through it all again.'

He said, 'I can't say I blame you. You're better off where you are.'

She chuckled. 'My word,' she said, 'you've certainly changed.'

He said, 'I suppose we all do.' He rubbed his face. 'I wasn't expecting you,' he said. 'Not here. I thought I'd travelled much too far away.'

'Oh,' she said, 'you know me, John. I'm the little crab who always hangs on. Remember?'

'Yes,' he said. 'I do.'

She was quiet a moment, watching along the canal. She said, 'This is a lovely place.'

'It needed you,' he said. 'It was rather pointless before.'

'Where were you going?'

He said, 'Hy Antiel.' He gestured at the bank. 'There were two of us. But . . .'

She said, 'I know.' She shook her head. She said, 'You haven't altered all that much after all.'

'What do you mean?'

'Poor John,' she said. 'You never could understand, could you? About other people.'

He said, 'I didn't want it to happen. I didn't want him to be hurt.'

She said, 'You never wanted anybody to be hurt. But you always forgot.'

He said, 'I'm sorry.'

She said, 'I know. It doesn't matter.'

A little silence. Then he said, 'Please come aboard.'

She laughed. She said, 'No, not now. But I will stay with you.'

He said, 'Thank you.'

She said softly, 'It's more than you deserve.'

He said, 'You were always more than I deserved.'

He let himself sink back. Later she too dozed, her head resting on her arm. For that he couldn't blame her. It had been a long way, from Tuonela.

Sunlight lay in hazy patches on the water when he opened his eyes. He sat up slowly, pushing back the fabric of the bag, and saw how clever she had been. The light patch of her skirt was bright grass seen through a triangle of lapping boughs. The smooth rootstock of a shrub had made her ankle; and she had used a glistening branch for the sheen of her hair. He moved, and she was gone. But there were many shadowed places on the canals, many quiet banks of grass; he found himself not without hope.

The shaking in his legs and arms was bad, but his head felt fractionally clearer. He started the engine, poled the boat from the bank. The canal was wider here and deep, curving gracefully beneath the overhanging bushes. The diesel chugged steadily; the wash ran slapping against earth banks studded with moss-grown holes. The *chikti* made them, the little burrowing mammals of the tropics.

Three miles before the flight a broad green arm of water opened to the left; the Coldstream branch, that once had served the villages to the south of Hy Antiel. He pushed the oar, leaning his weight steadily, watching as the bow began to swing. He had understood a final thing; that pain is life, and death is when the pain has gone away.

Ahead, the lapping of blue and gold repeated itself into distance. Beyond, dimly glimpsed, were the low hills of the watershed through which the canal, broadening and meandering, lost itself once more in the marshlands of the south.

WAGTAIL IN THE MORNING

by

GRAHAME LEMAN

One of the many valuable functions of sf is to point out dead ends and to examine ruthlessly the kinds of future no sane person would desire for himself or for his children. Grahame Leman has said he considers it an offence to be ideologically drunk in charge of spaceship Earth and the warning is too plain to be ignored. Only the fanatically blinkered and the rigidly misguided, surely, would condemn unpredictable liveware?

WAGTAIL IN THE MORNING

THE letter from the Ministry of Education was the first letter he had ever had in his forty-two years of struggle up the ladder. The envelope had been folded from a sheet of heavy, handmade rag paper and sealed with a wound of red wax at the meeting of the corners; his title and name, Dr. Hans Elberfeld, FBPS, had been written on the other side with a steel pen, apparently, in a free Italianate hand. The coarse texture of the paper between his fingertips, its weight, made his hold on it seem extraordinarily solid, made him feel more real by a quantum jump.

Dr. Elberfeld did not want luxury for himself: he knew too well that energy used at the sensuous periphery must be stolen from the watchful brain at the core, that his budget for his life could not allow such theft of energy; ever since his election to a fellowship of the British Psychological Society at the unusually early age of thirty-two had put him into the topstaff catchment area, he had been living in one room on beans and water. But this was a voluptuous moment, because he did very much want to be part of a circle that could afford, collectively, such contemptuous displays of the power and right to make waste: the waste of time, especially, involved in the preparation of a letter (from the laborious hand crafting of the paper and ink through to its delivery by a liveware courier, walking twelve miles across London in the rain, in his opulent livery), instead of having the words printed out on his home terminal in the ordinary way, shook him with a turbulent and delicious physical pleasure. It was almost an anti-climax to dismiss the courier, unseal the letter and read on the inside of the folded sheet that his security clearance and advancement to topstaff status had been confirmed, that he would be retained as a psychological consultant to the

Minister *sine die* and that the Minister would see him in locus 324.2 at 15.30 that afternoon.

He left his room in South London for Whitehall a clear hour before he really needed to leave, to be twice sure he would not keep the Minister waiting: he might be inside the periphery of the inner circle now, but he was still a very long way from the Ministers at its deep centre; although they are not formally marked in any way, there are as many rungs of standing inside the topstaff subset as there are labelled rungs outside.

With the letter crackling in his pocket, he went confidently through the free travel gate reserved for topstaff at the entrance to the tube station and straight to the marked stretch of the rapid transit platform which showed where the topstaff car of the train would stand, enjoying the new feeling of space around him.

The barefoot girl was in the crowd on the liveware section of the platform: at least, although he couldn't see her face or her bare feet, he thought it was her, because not many girls are so tall and red-haired as to look like an angry boil standing out of the skin of heads. She was usually on the train when he took the rapid to the West End, occasionally in the same car, and she interested him a little: perhaps because of his professional interest in the minor deviancies of comportment that were allowed to liveware as a sort of lightning conductor for their charges of frustration; perhaps in a rather more worrying way, since her bare feet (dirty, with broken nails, calluses, corns) disturbed him in a way he couldn't quite pin down, like the shop talk of his medical colleagues or speculation about strange forms of life on other planets of the galaxy. But there could, after all, be nothing wrong with *him*: he had his weekly preventive appointment at the council sporting house, and of course anything wrong with his conditioning would surely have glared from the Ministry's screening test results and blocked his security clearance and topstaff rating. He scratched the problem and, as the rapid drew away, began to think about a chapter of his book on the topology of nervous nets in the brain, which he was going to have to rewrite in proof to accommodate some anomalous experimental results from an obscure team of experimenters in Chile, already confirmed in Oxford.

Locus 324.2 was a confidential interview room in the social centre of the Min Ed complex. Since he had plenty of time in hand, he went to the luxurious topstaff washrooms, with their liveware attendants, showered, changed his underclothes, washed his used underclothes and put them in a plastic bag in his briefcase, brushed his teeth, used anal, underarm and oral deodorants, rubbed scented spirits into his scalp from the free bottle over the wash-basin, groomed himself and took advantage of the liveware manicurist. Although he did not need to use it, he was interested in the paper in the dispensers in the sit-down cubicles, which was certainly very thick and soft, and pleasantly scented: he was reminded of the sardonic remarks made by undergraduates, when they were undergoing their routine immunising exposure to subversive ideas, about administrative ability being inheritable in the germ plasm and invariably linked to inheritable sensitivity of the skin around the anus; he had often thought there might be something in that, since what the layman calls 'sensitivity' and 'a thin skin', which could well be inheritable properties of the nervous system, arguably predispose a man to a withdrawn attitude and to the life of the mind, favourable to success, while the more robust tend to get too involved with the world and with other people to be able to keep their cool and their concentration on what matters.

The Minister was a little drunk, or had perhaps taken barbiturates in rather more than the normal sedative dose. Elberfeld knew, had reconstructed from scattered indiscreet hints in the conversation of his clinical colleagues, that the so-called Berzelius syndrome was not uncommon in topstaff circles, and that its incidence was high enough to worry the topstaffers who didn't show it: Berzelius had been a systems analyst, who had cracked up spectacularly while running a USAF think tank in the 1980s and then written a maudlin, best-selling autobiography; in the book, he explained that he had done his clear thinking in the mornings while sober and had got drunk to do his own dirty work in the afternoons, so that his alcoholism was really a side-effect of his inability to delegate.

But the Minister's blurred bonhomie was pleasant enough; Elberfeld relaxed and listened:

'You're being invited in on the ground floor of a big thing, Elberfeld. What it is . . . well, Cabinet has decided that the hardware components of our society need no further development for the time being. As you must very well know, dear boy, from your colleagues in computer science, all the important bits are so small and cool-running now, that you can have as many of each whatnot as you need strapped in parallel to make quite sure they don't all fail at once, and everything is really as reliable as it need be. So we can switch the bulk of our available Research and Development heft to the liveware problem: the liveware, of course, is still dreadfully unreliable and unpredictable, and it is difficult to get things done tidily.'

'This is good news, indeed, Minister. We have been pressing for this for years, we psychologists, as you know. Why has it not been done before? The hardware, after all, has been on a high plateau for forty years!'

'Well, everybody presses for everything, dear boy. Whatever they do for a living, they have a natural feeling that the country needs more of it, so we don't pay much attention to that sort of pressure . . . don't worry, you'll pick up top-staff thinking as you go along. And then, Elberfeld, the experts usually disagree with each other, and it's not at all easy to know which one to believe: the fashionable ideas aren't always good, are they? Nor are the *un*-fashionable ideas necessarily any better. So we don't pay a lot of attention to expert advice either. The thing that usually decides us is news from abroad: we are very interested in what the big boys *do*. I sometimes think that we respect *their* experts more, simply because we don't pay them and don't get to meet them socially. Hah! Anyway, dear boy, we're going to follow the big boys, in case they're right, and switch the R & D heft to the liveware—after all, we should not survive economically for a year if they developed reliable and predictable liveware. Right?'

'Indeed, Minister. Yes, I see where I come in.'

'On the ground floor, dear boy, on the ground floor. You see, of course, that the power will come with the heft, across the river from Min Tech to Min Ed—because *we* run the liveware factories, the schools and colleges and so on. Within ten years, you could be the most powerful scientist in the country, Doctor Elberfeld, *if* you can prove yourself to us on the job.'

'What job, Minister?'

'You're very direct. I like that. Now tell me, dear boy, what education is *for*. Quick!'

'Bertrand Russell said it was a branch of the advertising business.'

'In your own words, Doctor Elberfeld. Quick!'

'Education is for the prevention of learning.'

The minister roared with laughter, slapping the table, sending gusts of chemically unpleasant breath into Elberfeld's face, showing a furred tongue and a lot of dental work in gold as he gasped for rasping breath:

'Excellent! You ... excuse me ... you can sweat a complex policy down to an epigram, which is a good topstaff talent. Now enlarge on it for me while I get my breath back.'

'Well, Minister, it's simple enough. No society can endure, or even work for a day at a time, if people can see what's in front of their noses. What education is *for*—in the home, in the educational plant, at work—is to make sure that this won't happen, that people won't be *able* to see what is pushed into their faces. This is possible, simply because we "see" most of our environment, so to say, "through" language—to be exact, "through" such structures made of language as lexical fields, logics, grammars, myths, creeds, philosophies, scientific theories. When you come to think of it, it is obvious that we can have no knowledge of anything outside the range of our five senses in the passing instant, which is *not* mediated to us in this way by systems of symbols: almost all our knowledge is of this mediated kind, only a vanishingly small part *im*-mediately sensuous. So, by careful manipulation of symbol systems, it is possible so to adjust the "sight" of the minds of liveware that they "see" the world in the way we want them to see it, in a way which will make them do what we want of their own accord, instead of having to be wastefully whipped or bribed. This, incidentally, is why it takes so long to train the expert liveware needed on tap by real people in the line of command: a prolonged educational effort is required to make a man stupid enough to be safe in a sensitive staff position, such as a professorial chair or a permanent post in the civil service, a consultancy in psychopenology and so on. If education does not prevent learning, it has failed.'

'Many, many thanks for the lecture, *Doctor* Elberfeld.'

'Believe me, Minister, I am not presuming to instruct you: I just want to show you that I have learned my lesson.'

'*Learned*, yes. How do you account for the fact that your education did *not* prevent you from learning? That seems to be a weakness in your argument, dear boy.'

'Nothing is perfect, Minister. My education didn't *take*—as your experts have evidently discovered from their tests, or I wouldn't he here.'

'You appreciate your danger, Doctor Elberfeld?'

'Of course. People like me must obviously be let *in* or eliminated: no middle way is possible.'

'Quite. The thing about *in*, dear boy, is that it is not exactly win or lose, as in the liveware circle outside: more like live or die—indeed, precisely live or die. But for people like you and me, Doctor Elberfeld—"real people", in your own words—it's the only game in town; we would rather be dead than out. But tell me, why does education not always "take"?'

'Mostly, I think, because our symbol systems are inevitably imperfect. Antinomies lurk in them, like the problem of explaining how a good God can permit evil, or the paradoxes of set theory in foundational mathematics. To the extent that symbol experts can deal with these antinomies at all, they can do so only by soaring to levels of abstraction so general that really nothing is being said, or something that succeeds in being both counter-intuitive *and* illogical: such as the blank assertion that all antinomies are resolved in the absolute, or belief in the subsistence somewhere outside space and time of an uncountably infinite set of real numbers in the interval between zero and one. There are analogues in political argument, which I won't discuss: though I will just point to, say, Aristotle's conclusion that there are two kinds of men, those born to be users of tools and those born to be used as tools; or the notion that inequities in society can always be dissolved in "growth", time without end. Again, Minister, I am not lecturing: only wagging my tail.'

'Good dog. Hah! Good *doc* ... I can make serious puns too, my dear Hans: we shall get along, we shall get along fine ... but *tail* is good ... mmm ... *tail* is good. Now, to business! I understand that there has been some sort of neurological breakthrough, or claimed breakthrough, in Chile in the Americas, which has caused major changes in policy both in the Americas and in the SU; and some people at Oxford, whom some say are competent, confirm the Chilean experiments. This, my dear Hans, is why you are here, rather than in the hands of the police.'

'I take your point, er ...'

'You can call me Harry, in private. Now get on, get *on*, man!'

'Well, Harry, people have for many years been playing around with electrodes inserted into the human brain, and it's well known that you can control a person's experience to some extent in this way: put your bit of platinum wire here, and you produce visual illusions; there, sexual pleasure; somewhere else, intolerable pain; and so on. Well, it immediately looked as if this was going to be the answer to the perennial liveware problem: Tanner, for instance, suggested that simple miniature radio receivers could be implanted inside the skull and connected into the nerve net, so that real people with transmitters could produce great pleasure or intolerable pain in a unit of liveware, simply by pushing a green or red button on a pocket transmitter, while mass control could be done by broadcast transmissions from a stationary satellite. As Tanner pointed out, this would be a way of making the old, unreliable, wasteful stick-and-carrot system completely reliable and economical: so that we could in fact go back to it, and get rid of all this complicated business of preaching religions like Marxism and Liberalism, cowboy series on television and the rest of the symbolic apparatus, and shorten the whole process of inculcation and maintenance of education by maybe an order of magnitude.

'Quite a lot of work was done on the rat, the dog and primates, and it turned out that there was a difficulty: the brain is not altogether rigidly structured, not all of its "programs" are "wired-in" like the hardware logic of a computer; new nets can grow even in the adult brain, as after injury, insult by a tumour, lobotomy and so on. Oddly enough, the individual brain is much less rigid, much more plastic, than a symbol system like mathematics or Marxism, which are hard to change because they are, so to say, *located* and held rigid in thousands of millions of brains, books, magnetic tapes and what have you. Now, an interesting thing about pain and pleasure is, that they are not—as might be supposed—irreducible physiological functions: higher functions of the brain *interpret* activities in lower parts of the brain as "pleasure" or as "pain"—morphine, for instance, is known to affect the *interpretation* of lower activity by higher functions as "pain", instead of affecting the lower activity itself. Well, to cut a long story short, it is just these higher brain functions which are most plastic: the brain adapts itself to the implants after a time and no longer feels "pain" or "pleasure" when stimulated by the implants. You follow me, Harry?'

'Perfectly, Hans. The trick won't work, because the brain

cunningly grows blocks, or bypasses or something in the net, so that the implants are isolated and ineffective. Right?'

'In the right parish. Frankly, we don't know if the brain grows new wiring, or re-programs itself without changing the hardware net, or if it can and does do either or a mix of both as required. But, somehow, it makes these implants ineffective—sometimes in a few days. At any rate, it *did*...'

'... Ah! This is where the Chilean work comes in, yes?'

'Exactly. The Chilean team were doing routine work screening new synthetic drugs for the property of giving major analgesia, in the heroin class, without producing addiction or dependence. They were working with pigs, and using implants to produce the experimental pain. One of the dugs they tried turned out to have the property of maintaining the effectiveness of the implant—in the longest series, for *twelve* years.'

'How, man? How?'

'Nobody knows. The Chileans lucked into it. Oh, there are *n* speculative theories, of course, but nothing beyond intellectual play: since we don't have the slightest idea how the brain isolates the implants, we naturally don't have any clues to what the drug might be acting *on*, so we're very much at sea.'

'But it works, Hans? It works?'

'It works, Harry. The Oxford group have done an impressive series with cats and chimpanzees, and they have already maintained the effectiveness of the implants in a group of chimpanzees for three years. Carter does very good work, and I don't think there's any finite risk that his results are shaky.'

'Yes. Well, Hans, what you say confirms what I've already been told. It means we can't ignore it, doesn't it?'

'Yes, Harry: it's like the atom bomb, we know enough to be sure we can't afford the risk of not getting it if it works. That's the size of it. And, in one way, we may already be ahead of the world.'

'How?'

'It so happens that Carter's group in Oxford have more experience than anybody else in the world in chemotherapy by implanting drugs in the body, so that they dissolve gradually and keep the body dosed. The Chilean drug, of course, is effective in vanishingly small doses, like some of the hallucinogenic drugs, so it would be possible to give a lifetime dose by implanting one pellet of the drug, anywhere where the dissolving drug would get into the bloodstream going to the brain. Stick it in a baby, and he'd be under the drug for a hundred years, if he lived that long. You see the implications?'

'My God, yes, Hans. If you implant the receiver and a pellet of the drug, the receiver stays effective for life. Completely reliable and predictable liveware. The millennium!'

'Quite. The only serious problem I can see is the economic problem. There would be a hell of a lot of surgery to be done, and . . .'

'Horse feathers! If we can provide every family with a car, sometimes two, and colour television, we can hack that without sweating.'

'But it would take years to train all the surgeons, surely?'

'Nah! nah! nah! You're one of the grown-ups now, Hans: you don't have to take that Royal College union stuff about twelve years training. If we want to train nurses' aides in routine brain surgery, in six-month crash courses, there's no sensible reason why we can't: Israel did it in the Nine Year War, and what they can do we can do in trumps.'

'I suppose you're right. But what about the liveware? Will they stand still for having things put in their heads, and in their kids' heads?'

'If it's the only way to get on, they will. After all, they'll learn Anglo-Saxon so they can get a piece of paper and go off to work in the advertising business. We'll introduce implants as a privilege for the middle classes: then, before we know where we are, the egalitarians will have forced us reluctantly to extend it to the lower liveware classes. No sweat, Hans!'

'But what about the real people? I mean, if everybody gets these things put in their heads, then there just wouldn't be any real people left to run things.'

'A good point, Hans. As Plato said, of course, there would have to be a class of Guardians: preferably an elective class, so that we get a self-perpetuating institution like the Church of Rome or the CPSU: these are much more stable than hereditary Guardian classes, because you don't have to take what the accidents of birth supply. It would be quite easy to put, shall we say?, slightly different things in *these* heads. It's the millennium all right, Hans, an endless age of impenetrable fraud, much to be preferred to the perennial pendulum-swings between fraud, violence and a new fraud welcomed by the exhausted combatants.'

'So what do we do now?'

'What you do, Hans, is to put together a team to develop this to feasibility; time matters, cost doesn't, you can crash-program it. I give you political support. And I'll see your first draft proposals inside a week, please.'

'Sir.'

'One more thing before you go. Doctor Elberfeld, do you know a tall, red-headed girl, goes about with bare feet?'

'I don't *know* her, even to speak to. I do often see her about, usually on the station and sometimes in the rapid, when I come up to the West End by tube. Why, Minister?'

'Mmmmm. Well, when my security people were investigating you for your clearance, they naturally followed you about a good deal. They say she was following you about too. No, we don't think she's an agent—or not in the usual sense. She belongs to a little group of kooks, quite well known to security, who are politically clean in the sense that they don't seem to be working for anybody but themselves and are too weak and incompetent to make real trouble. It's difficult to get too worried about an organisation that uses a six-foot redhead with bare feet as a tail, wouldn't you say?'

'What's this group's thing, then?'

'If it's crank, you name it and it's their thing. You must have seen the slogan they keep spraying on walls? No? It goes: "Your order is chaos: therefore there are explosions." Typical incompetence, it's much too long to stick in the liveware mind.'

'So she ... I mean, *they* are harmless enough.'

'Yes and no. Certainly, they're not going to put through a revolution: society is safe. But it shouldn't be beyond them to ... say ... well, push you in front of your tube train one morning. I don't like them showing an interest in you, just when you and your knowledge have become indispensable to us.'

'Are they likely to do anything like that?'

'Likely schmikely: who can tell with kooks? I'll tell you one thing though—that big redhead has published a number of poems and short stories, in little mimeo magazines, all with one obsessive fantasy theme: a blonde circus midget, who kills the ringmaster and lets the animals out of their cages. How does that grab you?'

'If they write it, they almost never do it: that's what writing's about.'

'But only *almost* never, dear boy. If there's a risk, however small, I think I'll pull that whole lot in and send them up to the change camp in Wester Ross.'

'On what grounds, Minister? Suspicion?'

'Nah! As there's more than one of them, we can always convict them of conspiracy. It's a good catch: the way the law of conspiracy stands, everybody is technically guilty of conspiracy if they have any social life at all. Now, be off with you, wagtail, and do some work.'

'Sir.'

As he left the Min Ed social complex, he saw the barefoot girl standing on the opposite pavement, outside a bank: she had one long arm outstretched, and a pigeon perched on the wrist was eating something from the cupped palm of the hand. Her red hair was tangled across her face by the breeze.

He walked quickly on, to the tube station, stopping often to look carefully behind him for a follower. On the station platform, he kept well back from the edge, against the wall, until the train was standing.

He slept fitfully that night in his austere room, remembering dreams in the waking intervals. Once, he had watched a surgical operation, green masks, overpowering clinical smell, heat of lights over the table: the theatre sister, with her board of numbered hooks for the bits and pieces, was four foot tall and bleached blonde; the surgeon had bad breath, and—when he held up the extracted tumour, stripped off his green mask and laughed triumphantly—gold teeth razzed in his mouth. Then attendants took the shrouded patient from the table, thrust it down a chute to one side into glimpsed flames, and the midget sister said through her green mask: 'Wonderful, Doctor Killdare—you've saved the cancer.'

At times he swam between the stars and galaxies, visiting strange planets. On one, great machines were silent, clogged and bound with red, blowing growths of some thread-like plant. On another, a slime mould as big as an ocean had eaten all the other living things of the planet and was slowly starving to death, distracting itself from the pain by developing abstract algebras from arbitrary postulates and seeing how far it could push them. Somewhere, a tricorn horse explained to him that the galaxies are mere neurons in the net of a great brain, connected by rivers of neutrinos, and a plastic man with only one eye gave him scientific proofs that the brain was mad.

Towards morning, he remembered parts of another dream. He was kissing some feet—dirty, with broken nails, calluses, warts, corns; he couldn't stop thinking about the huge population of bacteria on the skin of the feet, and he couldn't stop kissing them, so he tried to take his mind off the bacteria by making it dance the grave minuets of mathematics. She reached down, ten miles down, to put him gently away from her feet: she couldn't have him distracting her while she was feeding the hairless monkey chattering on her wrist. A blood red comet tail blew across her frown, streaming out to the end of time, and he woke up still worrying about the possibility that he had caught a disgusting disease and would have to be put down.

He was pleased to discover that this feeling was only a trace of the dream. The dreams, he thought, had had some mildly interesting structural properties: binary oppositions, mirror isomorphisms, reverse mappings and the like; it was really a pity that the *content* of dreams was so context-dependent as to be unamenable to any intellectually respectable mode of analysis.

On the dot of 0600, he got up; washed himself very carefully all over; brushed his teeth for twice as long as usual, as if specifying double-precision arithmetic; booked a personal call to Professor Carter at the Oxford Institute of Experimental Neurobiology; and began to pencil draft budgets, organisation tables and research programmes on the backs of the scratch print-outs he kept in a stack under his narrow truckle bed.

Outside the dormer window behind him, the sun rose bloody orange red in the chill morning mist.

MADE TO BE BROKEN

by

E. C. TUBB

There used to be a fad for jokes wherein aliens addressed Earthly artifacts of similar configuration to themselves with the resounding words: 'Take me to your leader!' When it comes to the real thing, however, as E. C. Tubb points out in this story where, further to complicate the situation, empirical and academic learnings clash, that's only the beginning of the problem.

MADE TO BE BROKEN

HEAD aching slightly from the effects of the hypnotute Lieutenant Zac Karsov made his way through the ship to where the landing party waited before the main lock. That he was late was no fault of his own, at the last moment Lieutenant Ku Buryia had developed an attack of acute appendicitis and was now lying cured and unconscious beneath the healing radiation in the sick bay. The ethnologist had demanded a replacement and Karsov was the only suitable type though why red hair and mongoloid features were so important he couldn't guess.

Hands checking buttons, insignia and weapon belt he made his way to where the little group stood waiting and snapped a salute.

'Lieutenant Karsov reporting for duty, sir!'

He had spoken to Gregg Haljan, another lieutenant but one of the planetary service and senior both in age and rank; but it was the ethnologist who answered.

'Lieutenant you are incorrectly dressed.' Susan Ward stood three inches below six feet and even the severe uniform of the Terran League could do little to hide the rounded curves of her figure. Blonde hair cut short framed a neatly rounded head and her lips were a spaceman's dream; but she had a cold, analytical mind and blue eyes to match. The general consensus of opinion among the younger men was that, as a woman, she made a good robot.

'You are bearing arms,' she explained as Karsov looked blank. 'You will please remove your weapon belt.'

Silently he obeyed. With the planetary rank of captain her word was law on everything connected with the contact and dealing with newly discovered races. Even so—he thought she was crazy. Haljan was old and she was a female which left himself and the three stalwart yeomen, all unarmed, to protect the landing party.

'That's better,' she said, and condescended to explain. 'Our purpose is to make peaceful contact with the natives and obtain their co-operation. If we bear weapons it will betray both our fear and our possible warlike intent, two impressions we have to avoid.' Without pause or change of expression she added, in the local tongue, 'I take it that you have been fully instructed in what you have to do?'

For a moment he looked baffled then, as his recently acquired education came to the rescue, answered in the same language, 'My teaching has been as good as the time allowed, Madam.'

'Try again,' she said curtly. 'You are talking to a superior therefore the title must be a prefix. Also your inflexion carries a negative connotation. The pitch should lift, fall then lift again.'

Dutifully be obeyed.

'Again!'

'Madame, my teaching has been as good as the time allowed.'

'Better,' she said reluctantly. 'Still not perfect but it will have to do. In any case I shall do all the talking.' To Haljan she said, 'Is the guide waiting?'

He sat outside, small in the screen, a slight figure enveloped in a dust-coloured robe. His skull was shaven and his face, what they could see of it, was completely devoid of hair. He looked as if he had sat there, waiting, for a dozen years.

'All right,' said Susan, reverting to English. 'You all know what to do. The three yeomen will leave first and stand, waiting, one ahead and the others to either side. Then you, Haljan, followed by myself and you, Karsov, at the rear. Under no account say or do anything unless it is absolutely necessary. You must understand that this is our first real contact with these people. The exploratory probe which discovered this planet did no more than land, test for environmental hazards, snatch a specimen, check for humanoid characteristics and brain-tape the language. The rest is up to us.'

Karsov cleared his throat. 'These people, are they human?'

'Yes. Probably the descendants of a group which left Earth at the beginning of the Great Expansion or even a splinter group from some settled world. That is why it is so important to gain their co-operation before they are discovered by the Outworld Federation. The League needs every ally it can get.' She nodded to the lock-operator. 'We are ready to leave now.'

Outside the sun held a gentle warmth and the air was rich with the scent of growing things. It was good air, clean, the slightly higher oxygen content inducing a subtle euphoria. Karsov inflated his chest as he followed the woman down the ramp, idly watching the sway of her hips before remembering to keep his mind on the job. Dutifully he looked around. The ship had landed in a clearing ringed with trees thick with blossom. The town, he knew, lay to the north hugging the banks of a river, within easy walking distance but invisible because of the forest. Lifting his head he looked at the sky, a clear blue dotted with fleecy cloud, the sun close to zenith.

As he reached the foot of the ramp the guide rose, took three steps backward and, with his hand held before his mouth, said, 'Oh, Mighty Excellencies, speak so that I may learn how to serve you.'

Susan said, harshly, 'Take me to those who rule.'

It was, thought Karsov, taking a hell of a lot for granted. For all she knew the man could have been a high chief waiting to greet the visitors from the stars and even his unused knowledge of the language told him she had used a contemptuous inflexion. Back home he wouldn't have used such a tone to a dog.

As they followed the guide he caught up with the ethnologist and said, quietly, 'Was that wise? I mean, you could have upset him. I thought we wanted to make friends with these people.'

Her nostrils flared with anger. 'Lieutenant, must I remind you of our respective ranks?'

'No, but——'

'You lack experience,' she interrupted. 'I do not. We are dealing with a primitive people, the very complexity of the language tells us that. No primitive chief would be unattended therefore this guide is a person of little account. A criminal, probably, someone who has no caste and certainly no pride. Having no pride he can afford to be offended for he cannot suffer hurt in what he does not have. Is that clear, Lieutenant?'

'I guess so,' he said slowly. 'But why need they be primitive? After all, if they are settlers from Earth, they must have retained something of their technology.'

'Not necessarily.' She was impatient and it showed. 'Cultures can regress, Lieutenant, or have you learned nothing in your travels through space?'

'Regress, true,' he said, controlling his anger. 'But so far?'

'Yes,' she said. 'I have no time to give you a lecture on ethnology, Lieutenant, but believe me, yes. Now regain your position, we are approaching the town.'

It was a small place as towns went, a straggle of low houses gaining height and obvious importance as they neared the centre where a multi-storied edifice reared. Behind it the houses shrank again until they reached the river where a mass of small boats clung to wharves. The streets were narrow, winding, yet clean enough with flowers blooming in beds to either side and more flowers bright against the walls, their roots held in boxes of coloured wood. Everything, Karsov noted, seemed to be made of wood, natural enough he supposed considering the proximity of the forest.

The streets were alive with people, men, women and the inevitable horde of curious children running bare-foot for the most part, brown bodies lithe as they scampered among the adults. The women were as tall as Susan and wore a simple dress which fell from one shoulder and reached to their ankles. The men were six inches taller, his own height, and wore tunics falling to mid-thigh, belted, the belts supporting knives and pouches. The hair of both sexes fell to the shoulder and both men and women wore jewellery, engraved bands of metal around wrists and upper arms, earrings, necklaces of pierced seeds, animal teeth and the separated vertebrae of fish. Facially they all seemed much the same; broad, flat, mongoloid features with dark eyes deep-set beneath lowering brows. Their hair was a glistening black and from them came the scent of vegetable oil.

Their guide halted as they entered a small plaza, backing, holding up his hand to shield his mouth.

'Oh, Mighty Excellencies, if it should please you to wait I will summon those you seek.'

'Lead on,' snapped Susan, in the tone she had used before. 'Make no further delay.'

Karsov frowned as they continued their journey wondering if the woman had made a mistake. She was too young to have had very much experience and he doubted if she'd had any. Real field experience, that was, not the theoretical problems set up by the classroom analogues. It was possible that in a system governed by rigid protocol points could be lost by making the initial approach but it was too late to worry about it now. Already they had entered the main square lying before the largest building which, logic told him, could only be the palace.

Before it stood a treble row of armed and armoured guards.

They were tall, their height accentuated by plumes springing from the crests of their helmets, robot-like in quilted padding, their faces masked, round shields on the left arms, long spears in their right hands. Barbaric, thought Karsov as the little group came to a halt. Decked and plumed and coloured like popinjays; but the spears were no toys and quilted armour had proven its efficiency too often for him to deride it.

As he watched a file of men came from within the open doors of the palace. First came a man dressed like their guide, another wearing an ornamented tunic and carrying a staff followed him, the third held a spear and wore a crested helmet, the one behind him carried a thing like an engraved disc surrounded by points, finally came a resplendent figure accompanied by two attendants each supporting one side of a panoply which sheltered the august personage from the sun.

The guards parted to let them through and, at Susan's order, the three yeomen fell back, Haljan with them, to leave her standing at the front.

To the older officer Karsov said, 'If there is trouble, sir, you grab the girl and I'll cover the retreat.'

'Orders, Lieutenant,' said Haljan tersely. 'Remember your instructions. Do not contravene them again.'

Snubbed, Karsov watched the proceedings, trying to ignore the prickling between his shoulder-blades and managing to keep his hand from groping at a non-existent holster. The two guides met and spoke to each other. They stepped back and the man with the staff approached.

'Who are you?' he demanded. 'From whence do you come?'

'From a far place,' said Susan. 'Bearing rich gifts for you all.'

Staff fell back and was replaced by spear. 'Are you warriors? Men of battle?'

'We are those of peace. We come in peace. We seek and offer friendship.'

Disc replaced spear. 'Do you worship the one true god?'

'We do.'

The power civil, thought Karsov. The power military and now the power spiritual. Pass them all and the next would be the big wheel himself. The King Elect or the King Divine or the All High, whatever his title might be he was the one with whom to do business. But the man who held the disc didn't seem satisfied. He was old, his face seamed with creases, his eyes narrowed as he stared over the rim of his emblem.

'Your voice is strange,' he said. 'High. Do all sound the same?'

Susan drew in a deep breath. 'Yes.'

Karsov flinched at the sudden howl of rage which broke out from all sides.

Captain Rayment rubbed thoughtfully at his chin as he stared at the three seated across his desk in the operations room of his vessel. 'So it was a bust,' he said. 'A washout. Is that it?'

'Not exactly.' Susan was defensive. 'We gained some knowledge and the next time we'll have greater success.'

'Haljan?'

The elderly lieutenant shrugged. 'Don't ask me, I'm an ecologist not an ethnologist. All I know is that something went wrong and we left that place on the double.'

'Karsov?'

'Our expert made a mistake,' said Zac. It would have been against human nature not to have taken his revenge. 'She obviously lacks experience in actually handling primitive peoples. Unfortunately for the success of the attempt she is a woman. Most primitive peoples have a taboo against women. Some things they can do, cook, bear children, weave, tend the fields even, but they are not allowed to participate in areas reserved for men. Primitives have no time for women diplomats. As soon as they discovered her sex they simply didn't want to know. Had she actually spoken to the big wheel they might have killed us all. As it was they simply ran us out of town.'

'So she broke a local taboo,' said Rayment. 'Well, that's understandable if annoying. Your recommendations?'

'I hardly think they will be of value,' said Susan impatiently. 'The Lieutenant is untrained in ethnology.'

'But he is trained in the use of offensive and defensive weapons,' said the captain flatly. 'He has also undergone a full survival course and one of the things about any spaceman is that he soon learns how to get along with other people. Lieutenant?'

'Miss Ward is a very attractive woman,' said Karsov imperturbably. 'As such she tends to be somewhat vain. A subconscious prompting, perhaps, but it is there. Unless she disguises her hair, learns to talk in a deep voice and wears a less constricting uniform she will always be taken for what she is.' He decided that he had been, perhaps, a little too rough. 'She isn't to be wholly blamed, of course. Within the League women have had true equality for so long now that I expect she simply didn't think about it.'

'Thank you for trying, Lieutenant,' said Susan, a little mollified. 'But you were right the first time. It was a mistake I shouldn't have made.'

'We learn by mistakes,' said Rayment. 'Is there value in the lieutenant's suggestion?'

'That I disguise myself?' Susan frowned. 'Perhaps, but there is something to take into consideration. They are sun-worshippers, that was obvious from the rayed disc and, anyway, most primitive peoples are. There could be ceremonies in which the body is exposed to the sun. Need I elaborate?'

Haljan grunted. 'Don't let us admit defeat before we've really begun. Do we have to participate in their ceremonies?'

'To gain their friendship, yes. If their spiritual life is strong, and if they follow the primitive pattern it is, then unless we participate we shall always be considered as outsiders.' She frowned at Karsov. 'You want to comment?'

'A matter of curiosity. Why did you insist that I accompany you?'

'I wanted to display a varety of differing racial characteristics so as to prove that peoples of divergent stock could work together in harmony.' She caught his expression. 'You disagree?'

'I think you are trying to run before you've learned to walk,' said Karsov deliberately. 'Not your fault, perhaps, theoretical knowledge can never be as good as actual experience and it could be that your instructors have grown a little careless. But in my experience no primitive race welcomes strangers. Xenophobia is a real problem to overcome. Of all the landing party I came closest to the natives as regards facial distinction. Dye my skin, fit me with a long, black wig, rig me in a tunic and I might just be able to move among them without arousing suspicion.'

'A spy?' Rayment frowned then nodded. 'It might work at that. Captain?'

'He lacks the necessary knowledge to make sense of any data he might obtain. If this society is taboo-ridden he would be bound to make mistakes. One of them might kill him.'

'A combined effort,' rumbled Haljan. 'Him to pry and you to teach. A miniaturised transceiver planted behind one ear and you to give instruction. The best of both worlds.' He chuckled, the sound echoing from deep in his chest. 'What is it they say? If you can't beat 'em, join 'em. My boy, you're going to do just that.'

A few hours later, trying to ignore the itching behind his left ear and the unaccustomed feel of air against his lower limbs, Zac Karsov left the ship and headed towards the forest. He did not head directly towards the town, unless the natives were totally lacking in curiosity there would be watchers, so he left the vessel on the far side intending to circle towards his destination.

As he reached the first of the trees a tiny voice carried by bone-conduction from the implanted mechanism said, 'Testing. Can you hear me, Lieutenant?'

'I can hear you.' The words were formed in his throat, dying before they could leave his lips. Man-made telepathy undetectable to anyone lacking instruments.

'Remember to report everything and anything you see. I shall not be able to advise you without full data to work on.'

'I'll remember, Captain,' he promised. 'And it's nice to know that you care.'

'For the mission, Lieutenant,' the voice said coldly. 'There is nothing personal about this.'

'A pity. With you I'd like to get personal.'

'Lieutenant!'

'Sorry,' he said, smiling. 'A sub-vocal wish, Captain. You shouldn't have heard it. Not that it wasn't genuine. As I said you are a very attractive woman.'

His smile widened at the answering silence and he could imagine how she felt. For once he had the perfect excuse to make a personal approach to a female of superior rank and she could do nothing but listen. He wasn't even contravening regulations because many men had consciously to avoid sub-vocalising their thoughts and she couldn't be sure that he wasn't one of them.

He lost the smile as he slipped among the trees. Primitive or not these people had to make their way on this world and though the conditions seemed gentle yet there would be predators as the necklaces of teeth proved. At first they would have had their technology to fall back on, but then, as time passed, the lotus-syndrome would have caught hold and the downward slide commenced.

On Telchis that would have been easy. The trees provided easily-obtained food, the river would be full of fish and, winters were probably mild. A small group, inbreeding, returning to nature, taking life easy for a while. Tomorrow would be time enough to dig mines, build factories, get down to the sweat and effort of building themselves a replica of what they had left. Tomorrow.

And each year that passed meant just that much forgotten; decades and the task would be frightening, a century or so and it would be impossible.

He hit the town at sunset, coming from the west so that the light would tend to dazzle any onlooker. A child ran from his path into the shelter of a woman's arms. Karsov smiled at her and lifted a hand in greeting.

'Good evening, Mother,' he called.

She frowned but responded, 'May the peace of falling darkness be on you.'

'Is your man at home?'

This time there was no response. With a glare she gathered up the child and vanished into her house. Dutifully Karsov reported the incident.

'Precision,' said Susan. 'She didn't trust you because you were imprecise. If you were asking for her husband you should have said "man of your bed", if for her father, "man of your mother's bed", if for her brother, "man of your mother's womb", coupled with some distinguishing characteristic such as, "man of your mother's womb who owns the heavy club", if for her eldest son, "man of your womb first to arrive", understand?'

'It's a hell of a language.'

'Primitive ones always are. Complexity coupled to precision. One of the first things we'll have to do once they accept us is to teach them Terran-English and before you ask me why it is because that tongue is one of the best developed for the expression of intangible ideas. It also has no rigid grammar and can be understood no matter how you twist the words and tenses. For example "I am the ship tomorrow catching" is as understandable as saying "I am catching a ship tomorrow."'

'Basic English,' he said. 'Eight hundred words and you can read, write and communicate.'

'That's right.' She hesitated and then added, 'It's getting dark. You'll be careful, won't you?'

'Risk not my neck I do intend,' he said. And walked smiling into the thickening gloom.

At dawn he attended the ceremony of the rising sun. It was a simple thing and impressive enough in its way, the assembled guards, the people, the priest with his rayed disc, the deep shout of welcome as the first rays of the sun gilded the top of the palace. There were no women in the plaza, the sun being male required the devotion and welcome of males only. If there had been a moon Karsov would have gambled that it would have been the prerogative of the females.

As the assembly broke up he lowered himself to his haunches and leaned his back against a carved wall. It had been quite a night. Without any means of exchange he had wandered the streets, once tempted to steal but warned off by Susan's insistence.

'Don't do it!' she'd said. 'You may get away with it or you may wind up dead. The risk isn't worth it.'

He had warmed to the anxiety in her voice.

Twice he'd dodged patrols and there had been a small beast like a dog he would have reason to remember. Uneasily he shifted on the hard ground, feeling the dirt through the tear in his tunic, the sting of the place where teeth had struck. About midnight his luck had changed, a house, blazing with light, had held what could only have been a wedding feast. Emboldened by hunger and needing to learn all he could he had crashed the party. The food, mostly vegetable, had been plentiful and there had been a limitless supply of a thick, noisome brew which held a surprising potency. Then he had staggered with others to the common lodging house of the single males.

Now he sat and nursed his head and wondered why men were such fools as to poison themselves.

'Lieutenant!' Susan's voice was a clap of thunder in his throbbing skull. 'Lieutenant, please report. Are you all right?'

'I'm alive if that's what you mean.'

'Trouble?'

'Only self-induced. You can make a note that, in one respect at least, these people are just like us. They tell dirty jokes at parties.' He paused then added, 'They drink, too.'

'Naturally. The art of brewing fermented liquids is as old as time. Please bring me up to date.'

Sighing he obeyed. The guards were more than just a ceremonial guard of honour. They were the élite and the aim of every young man was to join them. At night they patrolled the streets, acting as police and breaking up disturbances. There was a rigid caste system of at least five levels and no inferior could talk to a superior unless first addressed. The lowest level was that of the guide. His hair and eyebrows had been shaved, his eyelashes clipped and he had to wear the robe of ignominy until they had regrown.

Armed men took precedence over the unarmed. Women did not mix with men but children could go anywhere. Both sexes had communal quarters which they used between puberty and marriage and, as far as he recalled, there had been quite a bit of nocturnal coming and going.

'It fits,' said Susan when he had paused to ease his aching head. 'Most primitives have such a system—especially in warm climates. Did you discover any fresh taboos?'

The place was rotten with them. Those coming from light into darkness had precedence over anyone coming the other way unless they were of a lower caste in which case it was taboo to use the same entrance. It was taboo to watch a mother feed her child unless the man was a close relative. It was taboo to spit towards the east in the morning and the west after noon. It was taboo to conduct business during the hours of darkness.

'All right,' said Susan. 'Now comes the hard part. I want you to wander all over the city and try and discover how they feel about us. Also attempt to determine what other peoples are near, do they engage in warfare, what gifts would impress them and, most important, have they been contacted by the Outworld Federation as yet.'

'We know they haven't,' he protested. 'If they'd found this world they would never have left.'

'All information is of value,' she said coldly. 'Even that of a negative quality. Good luck, Lieutenant.'

Tiredly he rose, saw a guard moving towards him, his obsidian tipped spear at the level, and moved quickly away. Loungers were obviously not permitted to sleep facing the palace. Or perhaps loungers were simply not permitted. More damn taboos. For all he knew he had broken one just by leaning his back against that particular wall.

Ignoring the guard's call he dived between two houses and made his way towards the river. Stripping he plunged into the water, remembering his wig as he dived under and hoping the glue would hold. Both wig and dye remained and he soaked for a while in the limpid water, watching the boats and the men along the wharves. More boats arrived as he watched, coming from up-river, paddled by stocky men with cropped hair but with the same mongoloid features. Traders, he guessed, and took advantage of the confusion to leave the river, dress and mingle with the crowd.

At dusk he returned to the ship.

'It is obvious,' said Susan, 'that we are faced with a rigid, static culture which is self-perpetuating and will do its utmost to resist change. The language itself is a barrier against the assimilation of new ideas and the complex taboos actively disencourage all innovations. That, of course, is the real purpose of such taboos.'

Fed, washed, chemically rested, Karsov leaned back in his chair and looked at the rounded figure of the ethnologist. Beneath her make up her face showed signs of strain and he remembered that she had been on constant monitoring duty all during his absence.

Haljan said, 'Aren't taboos basically for the protection of the individual and society?'

'Initially, yes, but once established they work to protect the status quo. Our job is to break it.'

'And soon,' reminded Captain Rayment. He looked at Karsov. 'How about giving me a run down on what you discovered?'

'The culture is pretty wide-spread,' said the lieutenant. 'I can't guess how long they've been here but it's long enough for the language to have formalised and reading to be a lost art. Maybe the priests still have the ability to mull over any books they might have but the general population couldn't care less. As the population grows so new towns are established, groups of young men and women strike out and make new settlements, usually along the rivers. The metal ornaments we saw must be remnants of the original vessel but there is some gold probably found in the hills, loose nuggets washed from exposed lodes. They have a medium of exchange based on shells, and strong family groups which are more or less self-providing. The palace has the right to demand service and supplies based on a calculation of a family group's possessions. Building is done on a mutual aid system. Art is confined to woodworking and weaving with a little sculpture and pottery. Dyes are obtained by treating seeds and shellfish—the usual primitive pattern. They are fond of combat-sports and there is quite a bit of gambling. Entertainment is by singers, story-tellers, dancing and drinking.'

Haljan said, 'Do they possess slaves?'

'No.'

'Menial work is done by the lower caste then?'

'Mostly, yes, but they don't regard menial work as we do. There are simply things which need to be done. The women take care of the domestic arrangements and younger sons and old men gather fruits and such. Hunting is confined to elder sons and the elite.' He paused then added, 'They have a lot of spare time.'

Time in which to spend half a lifetime carving a panel, scraping at the hard wood with razor-edged shells, fabricating a thing of beauty created by love. Time to assemble and sort a multitude of seeds so as to match size and colour, shape and texture, piercing them, threading them to form curtains and hangings of intricate loveliness. It had been a shock to realise that the things he had seen could not be duplicated on the civilised worlds, that sheer economics dictated that only things which would be stamped or poured or mass-produced could hope to lie within the purchasing power of the majority. On such worlds craftsmanship had priced itself out of existence.

But at least, he thought, when their system had been smashed beyond hope of recovery, the natives would not be without resources. Their art work would command high prices on the ancient planets. He hoped it would be recompense enough.

'Primitives,' said Rayment. 'In a way I envy them. A simple life in a world without mystery, where everything has its place and a man knows exactly where he stands. But they're living in a fool's paradise. Unless we win them over the Federation will move in and we know what will happen then. Alienation, extermination, exploitation. They'll be slaughtered like animals and those that are left will be worked to death in the mines. With us, at least, they stand a chance. Not this generation, perhaps, but those that are to come. It's up to us to make sure they retain their world.'

Mother Earth gathering up her children, thought Karsov, but the captain was right, the League was the less hurtful of the available alternatives. And yet he wondered, if he were a native, whether he would thank the League for its interference. A closed society had its peculiar charm. It was something like the ship, a snug, warm, comfortable little universe where everything was ordered and a man knew where he stood. And men needed to belong, to be a part of something greater than themselves, to give their loyalty to a cause.

'You're dreaming,' said Susan. Karsov looked up and met her eyes. 'You're thinking of the "noble savage" concept and wondering if we are doing the right thing. Let me assure you that we are. Not because of what the Federation might do if we fail but because of the inevitable results of such a society and culture which exists on this world. You think that everyone is happy and content but you are wrong. You forget the frustrated innovator who is put to death or banished for breaking a taboo. The inventor who eats his heart out for lack of sympathy or support. The lower castes who must live in a kind of continual hell. We are going to save them from that.'

'Agreed,' said Haljan. 'But how?'

'The usual method. We will give them things which they cannot make themselves. Needles, awls, metal artifacts to which they will soon grow accustomed and on which they will rely. Then, when they need more, we will supply them at a price.'

'The worm in the woodwork technique?' Rayment frowned. 'Sure but slow. Too slow.'

'And it wouldn't work,' said Karsov. 'The big wheel has only got to set up another taboo—that of not taking gifts from strangers.'

Susan was defiant. 'They will break it.'

'No. The head man is regarded as the living personification of the sun and so is backed by the authority of a god. And if that wasn't enough his guards are. You haven't seen them as close as I have. I can assure you that those spears they carry make a telling argument—and they won't hesitate to use them.'

'On us?'

'On anyone who gets in their way. You're up against ingrained pride and stubborn conviction, two things you can't handle with kid gloves.' Karsov caught her expression of disbelief. 'Now listen to me! I can guess what you were taught at college, the liberal approach, the gentle way of going about things. You want to beg, to plead, to bribe with gifts and hope that they'll be so grateful they'll roll over and paw the air. It's not going to happen like that. You're trying to teach people a discipline they have no intention of accepting. They don't like discipline, not the harsh, real, universal cause and effect type of teaching. That's why they regressed. It isn't easy to learn to read, to build a civilisation, to have to think. It's easier and much less sweat just to ride from day to day and take what is going. And they have pride, remember. Act like a doormat and you'll be treated like one. No one with pride respects a beggar.'

'Are you trying to teach me my job, Lieutenant?'

'Did I say that?' He met her furious eyes. 'I spent a day among them. I listened to what they had to say about us. They think we're stupid, weak, commanded by a woman. Beggars pleading to be friends. You made an initial mistake and now they hold us in contempt. We've got to correct that impression before we can even hope to get anywhere.'

'And you know how to do that?'

'Well,' he said. 'At least I can try.'

The next time he headed for town Karsov was not alone. With him went a score of yeomen together with Haljan, all armed and dressed for battle. They reached the main plaza just as the welcoming shout of the dawn ceremony echoed from the surrounding houses and, before the assembly could realise what was happening, had forced their way to within twenty yards of the ranked guards.

'Lieutenant?' Susan's voice held a note of worry. 'Are you all right?'

'Everything is fine,' he said.

'If you make a mess of things we'll never get another chance,' she said. 'You realise that?'

'You worry too much,' he said, hoping her concern was for him and not for her record. 'If this is a bust we'll try somewhere else. Knock over one of these towns and the rest fall like dominoes. But we won't fail.'

'I wish I could be as sure of that as you are.'

'You can be. Sign off now, the welcoming committee is on its way.'

It was the same as before, a file of men coming from the darkness of the palace into the early light of dawn, the guards parting to let them through.

To Haljan Karsov said, 'No slips now. Arrogance all the way.'

Haljan nodded. As the robed figure of the lowest caste man approached he knocked him aside with a back-handed slap. The staff he ignored. To the spear he said, 'You offend the All High. It is taboo for him to be approached by such things of low caste.'

'And I?'

'You are a warrior and worthy of respect.'

'Are you also a warrior?'

'I serve the All High. He is the greatest warrior this world has ever seen. His power is such that he has subjugated the races of the men you see in attendance and yet each of them has more than all the people in this village combined. You are honoured that he condescends to permit you to stand in his presence.'

The man with the spear frowned, fingering the shaft of his weapon, ingrained pride struggling with the novel concept that he could be so lightly regarded. Before he could decide on a course of action Karsov stepped forward, contemptuously brushed him aside and stepped towards the king.

He heard the sharp catch of indrawn breath from the watching guards, Haljan's instinctive gasp of warning, and turned to catch the glint of sunlight on polished stone. He had expected the attack and was prepared for it. His left hand swung up and to one side deflecting the point stabbing towards his face and, stepping forward, he swung his bunched right fist in a hard cross to the exposed jaw.

Snatching up the fallen spear he held the point against the wizened throat of the king.

'Hail, brother,' he said. 'Call off your guards or our father the sun shall watch the spilling of your blood.'

'You would kill me?'

'What is the penalty paid by those who break the taboo of violence to the All High? Your man attacked me. The penalty of death is yours. Unless your guards drop their spears they and you will die together.'

Behind him Karsov heard the sharp bark of Haljan's command and could guess at the reaction of his men, the lifting and aiming of weapons which held power enough to destory the town. But the guards didn't know that and even if they had it wouldn't have stopped them. Only their supreme chief could do that and, watching him, Karsov knew that he wouldn't. Inbred pride made it impossible for him to beg for his life. He would die as he had lived, supreme in the eyes of his people.

And killing him was the last thing Karsov wanted to do.

For a moment he felt that he held a tiger by the tail, a product of civilisation faced with the bafflingly different mores of a primitive, and then did the only thing left for him to do. Throwing aside the spear he opened his arms.

'Brother! You are indeed a man! I, the eldest of our mother's womb, salute you!'

He smelt the reek of oil as he embraced the withered figure, the sudden easing of tension within the aged frame. To one side the priest lifted his rayed disc, his voice sharp with suspicion.

'You, man of a place far away? You claim to be a child of the sun?'

'What else?' Karsov released the king and whipped off his uniform cap, the sun shining on the red hair beneath. 'How can you doubt? Can you not see this sign?'

'You were lucky,' said Susan. 'Damned lucky. What if that spear had taken your life?'

'It didn't.'

'But it could have done. Lieutenant, you are a fool!'

But a lucky one, he thought, relaxing on the soft grass. Very lucky indeed. The more so because he and the ethnologist had taken a walk together to discuss what had happened and, somehow, had wound up among the trees in a tiny glade well out of sight of both natives and ship. He didn't think it was wholly an accident.

'You broke every taboo they had,' she mused. 'All except spitting at the sun. How come you didn't do that as well?'

'It wouldn't have paid to alienate their religion. I went as far as I dared when I grabbed the king. Don't forget he is their living personification of their god. Not that it matters now that we are friends. Equals, rather,' he corrected. 'Co-workers in the common cause.'

'To lift his people into the sun and share unimaginable loot.' Susan shook her head with mock despair. 'How could you lie to them like that? Don't you realise that they'll learn the truth eventually?'

'Truth is relative,' he said. His throat felt dry from hours of talking, explaining, lying, but he was satisfied. The breach had been made and the rigid structure of the local culture would soon fall apart. The Terran League had been accepted as guides, mentors and friends. Susan could chalk up her first real success.

'Thanks to you,' she said when he pointed it out. 'But how did you know what to do? At college they——'

'Talk a load of guff,' he interrupted. 'Textbook theorising

unbacked by actual experience. The biggest mistake they made was in teaching you to treat primitives as if they are equals. They aren't. As far as they are concerned they are immeasurably superior. To gain their respect you have to prove that you are as good if not better than they are. And that includes lying, stealing, fighting and anything else they set high value on. In this case it was fighting, arrogance and divine descent via the sun.'

'Red hair,' she smiled, and ruffled it. 'I should keep you around to advise me. Did you know that I was staying here until things are under control?'

'I'd heard about it.' He turned to look up into her face. 'I could get a transfer to the planetary service if you think it's a good idea. Do you?'

She coloured a little. 'You're forgetting something, Lieutenant. I'm of superior rank and it's against the rules of the service for a man of lesser rank to make a proposal to a female of a higher.'

'I'm due for promotion.'

'Even so——'

'Regulations,' he said. 'Taboos. To hell with them.' Reaching for her he held her close. 'They're only made to be broken.'

THE ETERNAL THEME OF EXILE: THREE ENIGMAS II

by

BRIAN W. ALDISS

Here are three more of Brian Aldiss's Enigmas—glittering dominoes masking the faces of human experience and exile and the agony of eternal farewell. Brian Aldiss has recently completed his mammoth investigation into science fiction, The Billion Year Spree, *and its publication marks an important stage in the evaluation of sf.*

THE ETERNAL THEME OF EXILE: THREE ENIGMAS II

THE ETERNAL THEME OF EXILE

ANNA KAVAN believed that I was persecuting her. Rather, she believed that she was being persecuted and that I was in some way responsible for the persecution. Sometimes, I was the chief agent of it; sometimes, I was no more than an innocuous bystander who acted as a focal point through which some insidious form of vengeance was channelled.

In order to prove to her that I was entirely innocent, I decided one morning to travel to the Outer Zodiacal Planets. My secretary informed me that an ion-jet was leaving for OHG 3RL in an hour's time. I registered with the Ministry of Slavery and checked aboard the I. J. 'Silence' as a Propulsor.

We arrived at OHG 3RL, a distance of sixteen point four light minutes, fourteen minutes later. Resuscitation took a little over half-an-hour, and then I was allowed on to the face of the planet.

One never becomes used to the changes in metabolism which take place as one treads ground which is not Earth's, not even when one has travelled to as many exotic scenes as I have. On OHG 3RL. I was burdened with the miseries of an entirely imaginary past, details of which, crowding in on my senses, almost drowned out what I thought of as my normal personality.

The impressions were so evanescent that, once I left the planet, they could never be recaptured. I retain a memory of them only because, as it happens, I stopped at a booth offering narcissistance and made a cassette of my troubles.

'Father, I still grieve that the state closed down your business just at a time when, in middle age, you were at last making a success of your life. We were so proud of you, your ailing family. We too felt the bitterness of an edict pronounced just because our skins were of a different colour from our neighbours. Our hearts bled for you—mine particularly, because Erik and Franz had their own jobs, whereas I, your youngest, worked only for you.

'Now that you are dead, I realise how bitter you were that you could no longer provide as head of family. Perhaps it was a mistake that we left the country and went to start life anew in K— in Africa. We always held the move against you, hating K— as we did. Only now do I see how truly you hoped for a freer life for your sons, unable to understand how your bitterness was imprisoning us all in your old European world we seemed to have fled.

'The constant journeying broke Mother's health. First the slow boat down the East Coast, calling in at all those squalid ports. Then the attempt to settle in Johannesburg. Well, we were happy there for a while. That was where I first saw Anna. Then the two-year trek north, the succession of horrible vehicles...'

So the catalogue went on, always with the eternal theme of exile—one perhaps nearer to the human heart even than love and hate. All the while, I earned a slender living working in the great earth kilns of Kubanjitully, the capital of OHG 3RL. I knew I had to live there for a year. Then I could return to my native planet. So great were the relativity gradients on OHG 3RL, owing to the Black Class sun, that when I set foot again on Earth, Anna would be an old lady, and no longer in fear of me—if indeed she remembered at all.

The year passed. I laboured through it with many lifetimes on my back—not only mine but those of a bedridden mother, rambling on about her idyllic childhood in the Ukraine, and of my brother Franz and his wife and two children, all of them completely imaginary. Franz lost his job because of his inability to master the complex atonal language of OHG 3RL; he drank and soon became unemployable. His wife, Hettie, a wan and consumptive girl, more and more sought my company.

At last, I returned to the space port and registered for passage to Earth. As I was boarding, Hettie ran up and begged me to take her with me. Compassion and lust made me agree. In a moment, she was crowding into the cryobunk by my side. Our joint decision was to settle in New Zealand, there to forge a happier life together.

Earth again. My old personality hardly fitted me. I came down the ramp alone, conscious of irredeemable loss. What had I dreamed? I looked up, but heavy cloud covered the night sky. Every star was a life, so they said.

'Well, at least there was Anna. She would be old. She would be at my mercy. To all my old armoury of tortures, I could now add the fact of my youth.

I bought a pale flower for my buttonhole.

ALL THOSE ENDURING OLD CHARMS

To escape the attentions of Anna K—, my master journeyed to the Remade Planets, where he served his time as a demographer in the state of Aphos, on Caphoster. He took on to his staff two beautiful young females, whose names were Vittoria and Venice; their job it was to classify data and tend my master's Madagascan Indris.

The Remade Planets had been in existence in their present form for many thousands of years. They had been set in orbit about Profabdos; there were sixteen of them, most of them burnt-out cores of old suns. On Caphoster, most of the states specialised in one predominant emotion. My master had chosen the state of Aphos because its predominant emotion was severity, which was congenial to him.

'Tomorrow, we visit Hostas, the city beyond the Tiger Glacier,' he told me. 'You will accompany me. Vittoria and Venice will remain here with the animals.'

The Tiger Glacier was so called because of the stripes that ran along much of its length, painted by moraines brought down from the mountains. We crossed it in a day and found ourselves in Hostas, a strange city where one sailed over magma to get from house to house. No windows were built into any of the buildings, in order to keep out the permanent drifting smoke. It proved a congenial city to my master, he sinking quickly into its vices and duties, investing in its fashions and obsessions.

During our second year there, he came across his own name carved on a memorial. After extensive enquiries, he discovered that Hostas was the city of his family's origin, or had been, several thousand years earlier.

'Send a message to Vittoria and Venice to come at once,' he told me. 'We will reside here for a term. There are connections I must explore.'

No sooner was the message sent than he made another discovery. The cryotomb of his ancestors stood in another part of the city. Indeed, it had been added to within recent date. After application to the city fathers, my master entered the cryotomb; there he found his grandmother in DSA, clutching to her side an immense lily as she endured phases of minimum biological activity.

Busy although he was, he decided to fall in love with her and have her reanimated. No doubt he was attracted by the perversity of the idea, while the fatal disruptions in his family, dating from early in his father's lifetime, probably encouraged his intentions.

By the time the necessary papers came through, and the tomb was set to Regeneration, Vittoria and Venice had arrived in Hostas. Celebration was in order. All my master's new friends came to see how beautiful the girls and their animals were, so that other projects were forgotten for a while. The Festival of Enshrouding Smoke was held, commemorating the original programming of the city.

My master was in a tavern on Culpice Street when he saw his grandmother on the other side of the room.

'My faith, but she resembles Anna,' he said. She was haggard but still possessed charm, despite her advanced years. She had been endowed with a fine bone structure; it was simply that this same bone structure was now more prominent than formerly. Unfortunately, she took offence at the sudden amorous advances of a hitherto unknown grandson, and would have nothing to do with him.

Daily, my master sent her one lemuroid after another, hoping to win her heart. One by one, the animals were returned, decapitated. My master sent her flowers, mathematical disputations, five-dimensional objects, sweetmeats, metaphors, plumes, plums, live jewels. All were returned. Grandmother was not to be moved.

'How vexatious,' said my master to the girls, 'that I should leave one planet to escape the attentions of a woman, only to find myself on another planet where another woman plainly wishes to escape my attentions!' He besought Vittoria to go to his grandmother and present his case personally. Vittoria was not returned.

Venice now begged my master to forget his madness, relinquish his exile and head back to Earth. Such were the charms of his grandmother—in his eyes at least—that my master would agree to this only if Venice would go first and make one final attempt to convey his feelings to the romantic old lady. Resignedly, Venice went. She was never returned.

Overwhelmed by amusement as well as remorse, my master wrote an elaborate suicide note to the elusive charmer; he then relinquished his post as demographer, and we left the Remade Planets.

But he remained attached to his beautiful suicide note, which seemed to embody for him many of the eternal truths of love. On the voyage home, he recast it as a love letter, posting it to Anna K— as soon as we docked in Tellus City.

Nobody Spoke Or Waved Goodbye

No, I was never in love with the man I still call 'my master', not even during those few months when we were married to each other. Differences in ages, temperament, position—especially the fact that we had been born on different planets—all such things make us completely incompatible.

Why, then, am I never free of him?

Only today he was here, as ever more keen to be clever than kind, bringing with him that blank-faced clone-serf of his.

'Anna, I'm leaving tomorrow. I came to say goodbye.'

'Where are you going? Back to Caphoster?'

'Ten years in DSA. I'm hiring out my personality while I'm gone. If you have patience, life can teach you a lot about the human condition you'd never understand in any other way.'

Always those baffling remarks of his. I would not kiss him. He left me his silver coffee service, many volumes of Anna Diary, some anatomical studies, gutta percha figurines, foils, veils and an eidetic dream-memoriser. Despite which, I felt myself alone.

Consolation was something I always found in the melancholy Masked Gardens of Santarello. I chose a lemur mask and walked along the wall.

The eternal conspiracy had penetrated even there. Among the crowd, someone spoke my name. Soon it was taken up on all sides. I ran among the trees, dropping one of the volumes of Anna Diary as I went. Someone would find it with all its vile explicitness; their life and mine would be ruined.

I sank under a chestnut tree. A short-haired man stood there, smiling.

'I can tell you are a hunted being,' he said. 'But at least you live at the centre of your world; people find you worth persecuting. I live only on the outer perimeters of my existence, a nomad unfit for persecution. My spirit is grey, yours cerulean.'

Faintly, I said, 'Please go away; I can tell your personality is hired.'

Although I absorbed myself in my work, and in particular in a town I was redesigning in Wildgreif, my emotional life was empty. Some months later, I met the smiling man again.

'Are you still on the perimeters of your existence?' I asked boldly.

'Working towards the outer suburbs. I find you in my subtopia, in uncertain light.'

'Cerulean no more?'

'The human face is the most spectacular of all objects. Yours includes much of the sky.'

We became lovers before I discovered that, in his double life, he was famous. Wherever he went, crowds of short-haired men and women followed him, all more handsome and youthful than I could tolerate. I asked him what he could possibly find in my small pale being on which to nourish himself.

'Only surprise me!' Sometimes he quoted obscure poetry.

When I began evading him, he followed me to Wildgreif. I computed his face obsessively into the façades of public buildings. Every gesture he made could be expressed in the rhythms of thoroughfares and traffic-flow lanes. His hired characteristics I expressed in the tensions of bridges and spaceways. To his persecution of love I supplied an answering persecution of function. Soon he was pervaded by interpretations of himself; the whole city became his anagram. The original population moved out, while all his followers moved in, delighted with the fantasy of existing within the spirit of their hero made concrete.

His will broke before mine. 'It is well to remember that evil is a pretty bad thing,' he said. 'I shall leave tomorrow for the Outer Zodiacal Planets. In any case, my present avatar expires next week.' He moved 1·03 light minutes away, but I could still see him.

All his admirers came to the spaceport to see him off. Nobody spoke or waved goodbye. There were ashes in the air, and traces of older destinations.

Now someone else wears the hired personality. My city expires under its borrowed mannerisms, like machines whose wheels are velvet. My master sleeps for another seven years. I age. Shortly, I will revisit the environs of the Paranoid Sun, and then again dreams will be worth the memorising and vitamins will fall from the atmosphere.

Meanwhile, I preserve my taste for the curious. A fame of my own has come my way; the lost volume was published, to immense acclaim. Now, on buildings expressing his animus, I find my anatomy sketched. Time has many revenges, but seven years will not pass too soon.

All that I was, he is. All that he was, I wish I were. As long as he remains asleep, I remain in exile; the foils and veils cannot comfort me.

THE FIVE DOORS

by

MICHAEL STALL

Tests notoriously bring out the best and the worst in people and in priding ourselves on always rising to a challenge we are aping our ancestors. However deplorable or anachronistic such a stance may be, it could come in mighty handy . . .

THE FIVE DOORS

The First Door

Inspector Norman Williams of the Humberside constabulary rubbed a rather too bristly chin with his uniform black glove as he looked on the long metallic cylinder that had sprouted overnight in John Sternson's field. It certainly looked solid and substantial enough: it was surely no hoax; but that being so, just what was it?

'There's an opening at the other end,' Sternson told him and Williams turned to look at the anxious farmer. But it was no use asking him any more questions; he could either wait for the arrival of a superior officer, or he could investigate himself. There was no question in his mind of what he ought to do; the Humberside constabulary was just five years old, as old as the new county, but in that time it had established the usual traditions.

'Lead the way.'

The opening looked dark and forbidding, and it was quite impossible to see any distance into the object. Williams looked back at the road, two hundred yards away, where he had ordered his driver to remain in the car, in touch with local headquarters. Perhaps he ought to tell his driver... But tell him what?

'Wait here,' he told Sternson, and started in.

As he entered, he took off a glove and felt the metal; it was cold to the touch, and smooth—very, very smooth. Some alloy or other, he thought, as he went from the dark portal through a dark passageway, to enter a small, brightly lit chamber, with faceted walls that for a moment made him think he was stepping into the interior of a cut diamond. He touched the glistening wall, and this time it felt warm and yielded a fraction to his touch—but no more. And there was a soft, rustling noise behind him.

He turned quickly about to see the chamber wall parting. He moved into a defensive crouch; but nothing more happened, nothing emerged from the new door, and the passage it opened on was as dark as the passage by which he had entered. Instinctively, he turned the way he had come, half-expecting to find that way out no longer available to him. But it was there, just as before.

In a flush of courage, inspired by the barely conscious realisation that only by action would he have an excuse not to think too deeply about the nature of the thing he found himself in, he entered the new passage with a brisk step.

The passage ended in a glittering screen that shone like the diamond walls of the chamber; but as he approached it he could make out a picture, a scene beyond it. Green pasture and trees, and about a hundred yards past the entrance, another cylinder, shining in the sunlight.

He pressed forward through the screen which offered no resistance, as if it were an illusion; and he stood on green grass, beneath a blue sky. But it was an alien sky; the grass wasn't the right colour of green; it was strangely bifurcated; the trees were such as had never grown on Earth; and the air had a strange, metallic taste to it. And none of it bothered him. There was a bucolic peace to this landscape; there were no signs of handiworks or artifacts; and everything, for all its strangeness, felt right.

He pressed forward to the new cylinder thinking, even as he entered it, that the chamber within, if it resembled the one he had just come through, was too high to be accommodated—as it was—in the cylinder.

Inside it was as before; a new passage opened for him; he entered, and as he approached the screen, he began to make out the view of a different, dark world, all rocks and shadows. He put forth a hand to where the screen seemed, and felt nothing. Then he withdrew it. He had come far enough; he had learnt enough, perhaps more than enough, for the present. It was his duty to return and report in safety ... He turned and made his way back under that safe though alien sky, beginning to wonder what it would be like to be famous.

The Second Door

As he lumbered over the grass in his radiation suit, Dr. Julian Wechsler found he couldn't concentrate on the great enterprise he was about to undertake; he just felt ridiculous under the gaze of the red-tabbed generals and senior civil servants dotted about the field. Who was it who'd said he didn't believe in adventure because even in its midst, one was always onself? He couldn't recall; all he could think of was that he felt itchy inside the suit.

He was actually glad to enter the passage and make his way into the chamber, where there were only three tunnel technicians who saluted him wordlessly as he entered the second passage.

It had all been so much easier for poor old Williams. He'd talked to him in hospital before he'd died, and been very struck by the description of the other world, of the walk Williams had had there, of the peace he had felt there. The peace, though he had not realised it, of a dead world. They were only now beginning to know; but it looked very much as if all the sentient life of that world had been destroyed in some atomic war. It would be easier to tell when the new batch of radiation suits were ready. But for the time being, of course, they had to concentrate on the second door.

He stopped at the screen and picked up the radiation counter that lay just before him. He checked it with practised ease and then began the long walk through the lead tunnel that had been mechanically extruded to join the two cylinders so that in future it would be possible to pass between them without all the ridiculous garments that he now wore. That was essential if the apparently airless world the second door led to was to be properly explored.

He watched the needle on the central dial carefully as he walked; if it started to swing the wrong way he would know that the seal wasn't perfect and get back in double quick time. But it held, and he found himself in another chamber, just like the one he had left.

Strictly against instructions, but just as he had intended, he walked down the new passage, and looked out on an airless world. In the distance he could see another cylinder. But it was someone else's job to get to that. And a much simpler job than his own, he judged. His team had done a good job. It was time to go back and tell them.

The Third Door

Ernest Thorton screamed. No one heard the scream through the thick full-protection suit, but the young doctor just saw the open mouth and guessed the pain. It was not hard to guess when one saw the fungoid growth that had been Thorton's face. The young doctor took out a syringe, but his older colleague stopped him. The outside of the suit had been sterilised and sprayed with sealer when he had crawled back through the door; now, they could not take the risk of allowing anything to get out, even through the smallest aperture. The young doctor nodded. The patient would be taken back through the airtube on New Moon to the second chamber. There they would decide whether it was safe to take him back to Earth. By then he would almost certainly be dead.

Ernest Thorton was still screaming as they began to move him.

Julian Wechsler scratched his chin. It was not one of his usual reactions but the request that had just been made of him in the domed, airtight resthouse on New Moon had nothing of the normal about it.

'Yes, I suppose the cylinders would stand it. No temperature we've been able to create has had any effect on them, but...' He shrugged. 'Who knows?'

'It's the only way,' Hardy insisted. 'Napalm has no lasting effect. An A-bomb mightn't have a very lasting effect either, but it would clear the hundred yards between cylinders just long enough.'

'Whose decision is it?' Wechsler asked him.

The grey haired spore biologist looked back at him hard. 'You could swing it. I mean, who is in charge of all this? The PM certainly. His nominee—just an elderly civil servant without scientific training. The real directorship of the project is up for offers. Decide on this, and it works—who else but you will be confirmed Scientific Director?'

The argument had a certain logic to it. The device—in both senses of the word—was crude, but it should be effective for all that; and Wechsler, otherwise a section head at a covert AWRE, was ambitious enough. The Scientific Directorship would eventually bring him a knighthood, a real footing in the scientific power politics of his country, of the world ... He nodded.

Hardy smiled. And suddenly Wechsler wondered at his motive. It could be pure scientific curiosity. It could also be that he intended to steal the credit for himself. Well, he'd picked the wrong boy for that. Wechsler knew he was only a middling physicist, but he was a damned good politician; he owed his present position to that. The thing to do, he knew, was to go straight to the nominee director and offer him the credit—he'd be only too willing to reward him with the Scientific Directorship: the inefficient always need good subordinates—his long service as a civil servant had taught him that.

The Fourth Door

Korner ran his eyes lazily over the array of instruments by the greenly flickering screen. The dials on the probe and back-up probes were all large and luminous as it was necessary for them to be read at some distance. The casts themselves were about the size of frying pans: if the next environment were radioactive there would be no large metallic objects to obstruct the way to the next cylinder.

No one, after Williams, was likely just to volunteer to

step outside in ignorance. It would have been better if the probes which were to be cast by a small spring steel arbalest, could radio back information. But radio didn't work. Before the screen and beyond were two different worlds.

It was nearly time. It was scheduled to start in ten minutes, and Director Wechsler was to be there to supervise. Korner wasn't too happy about that; he rather despised Wechsler as a time-server made good, but he had to admit the man had guts, and he certainly didn't want his job. He tried to lose himself in the mechanics of his own job in the project, but every so often he couldn't stop himself from thinking about the purpose behind the cylinders. With two men already dead, he didn't view the makers of this puzzle, or whatever it was, as purely beneficent. He even favoured the idea, current in the project, that the investigation be internationalised. But that was a dead horse; only failure would entail that, so he could not wish for it.

'Ready?'

Korner turned to see Wechsler standing in the passage. He nodded.

'It looks all right out there. Perhaps this will be a good world.'

Wechsler didn't speak, but his silence was a reply; it confirmed Korner's true opinion. Somebody would die out there. Perhaps himself.

'Let it go,' Wechsler ordered.

Stooping, Korner released the arbalest.

And it was all right! This was the good one, Korner felt, as he read the instruments, irritated by seemingly imaginary flashes of light at the edge of his vision: he had hardly slept in several days; sleep would put it right.

The re-fashioned, armoured, general purpose suit felt even more uncomfortable than the earlier version: Wechsler felt like nothing so much as a hastily fabricated tank, with himself doing duty as commander and powerplant. He would, he decided, memo the design team about the dehydrating unit.

Abruptly, he realised he was thinking about the suit so as not to think about what he had to do. Well, the best way not to think about it was simply to do it. Without another glance at his back-up man he stepped through the screen into the afternoon world.

He immediately felt ridiculous, like a knight in armour at a garden party. This world was different; but it was right. One could live here. This was the big one.

Something caught at his ankle. He shook it off without looking down. The second cylinder with its new door was only seventy yards off. Something was catching at his ankle again. It was like a large grasshopper. But in steel. And with appalling swiftness, the air was full of them, and they began to settle all over him. Not grasshoppers—locusts! He stood immobile, in shock, listening to a new grating noise—the sound of a hundred tiny steel pincer jaws eating away at his armour. Like a fly in molasses, he turned back the way he had come. Behind that door was safety, a back-up team, only thirty yards and how many parsecs away? A steel locust obscured his vision; all he could see were pincers gouging into armour glass, desirous of doing the same to his eyes. He wanted to scream, he wanted to run, but that would be death. Summoning all the self-possession he had, he began to walk slowly and deliberately back to the door, the grinding as his armour was slowly eaten away sounding like a death rattle in his ears.

He found the passage with his hands, just as the armour on his left gauntlet gave. He felt steel cut into his flesh. He screamed, but kept on. The armour broke in other places; steel teeth began to eat him alive, and still he moved on, until his counted paces told him he was at the door. He had to be there; his strength was at an end. Then he fell through, into the darkness.

A lecturer in Heuristics—a philosopher. A sounding board. A way of externalising a dialogue with himself. He had thought that; but it wasn't turning out that way, Wechsler realised. Gordey was taking over. It was as if the pain had bankrupted his mind. But he could not admit to that. He picked up the now lifeless locust from his bedside table—his hospital room was on New Moon, but from its appearance, it could have been anywhere on Earth. He turned the locust over in his hands.

'Utterly dead, now,' he said in a low, tired voice.

Gordey twisted in the visitor's chair. 'But how?'

'You've told me already,' Wechsler said. 'Either the door cut it off from its power source, whatever that may be, or the force screen that must somehow be incorporated in the door somehow deactivated it.' He shook his head tiredly. 'How does that get us any further?'

'You're viewing the problem in isolation,' Gordey said. 'The doors are a whole, a series of graduated tests. Until now, our technology has been up to it; now it isn't. So the problem is bringing it up to this new standard.'

Wechsler looked hard at the locust. Perhaps half a dozen new technologies were there, waiting to be taken.

'The project needs broadening,' Gordey said. 'It's too big for one country; perhaps for the world. We should——'

'No.'

Gordey nodded his submission to political reality.

'So be it. Then the thing is to decide what stopped the locusts. We can take it for granted they've eaten a sentient race out of existence, that they're programmed for just that. Every world, even this airless one, with its atmosphere blown off into space by God knows what weaponry, once held living intelligence.' He noticed Wechsler flush. Everyone on the project knew this; they just didn't like to talk about it—eminent scientists and superb technologists awed by the cylinders like medieval peasants in a great cathedral. But this was no cathedral, and Gordey refused to be awed. The makers were a long way from gods. He knew where he was. He was in Bluebeard's Castle and the fifth or sixth or seventh door was death for humanity. He was certain that was the intent; and he knew in his bones there was no turning back. The test couldn't be ignored; it had to be passed, and beaten.

'We'll concentrate on the force field aspect,' he said with as much assurance as he could manage. 'The doors have to incorporate them, otherwise air would rush out into the vacuum, or spores drift through. And the force shield we'll assume beat the locusts.' It was a tall order. But they knew they existed, so they could be understood and duplicated. And then the project would be the paramount power on Earth, for what importance that now had. And suddenly Gordey realised he was making a bid for power. Wechsler, lying half eaten on his bed, realised that too, that much was obvious.

'Well?'

With equally obvious reluctance, Wechsler slowly nodded his head.

Korner enjoyed using the shears. There was an element of danger about it; one had to get fully suited and lug the apparatus out to near the end of the passage, beyond the door; and the shield embodied in the shears was crude compared to the one in the doors: it flashed blue and green and yellow fire like a vastly expensive firework, was energy expensive, and the apparatus was constantly under repair.

But for men in armour it provided a way across to the next cylinder. And back on Earth—a long way back now—the project could use the field to make nuclear weapons obsolete. If the cylinders let men have the time. That particular thought was on everyone's mind. It was nearly two years now since the forward cylinder had first appeared in a Humber field; and there was a time limit to every test. Korner almost shivered as he thought about it. That was Gordey's view, and it had diffused downwards.

A pebble tossed through the door tapped against his armour. That was the latest communication system through a thousand kiloparsecs—that was the astronomical section's conservative estimate—and it meant the Deputy Director was coming through.

He worked the shears in a pyrotechnic display to clear the ground again. It was better not to use the shears with anyone in the way; that tended to build up a static charge on their suits.

As it happened, he didn't need to use the shears again that day: Gordey crossed uneventfully.

The Fifth Door

With Wechsler slowly being put back together again with grafts and cosmetic surgery on New Moon, Deputy Scientific Director Gordey ran the project: the titular head sat in an office in London and signed requisitions, or authorised someone else to authorise someone else to do the same. As he stripped off his suit, he vaguely wondered at the mechanism that kept *here*—without the intervention of mankind—at a sufficient heat, and with a proper partial pressure of oxygen. They didn't even know how that was done yet, or where the doors got their power from. He pushed the thought out of his mind and looked about him.

The back-up team on door five was the largest for any of the doors; there was no forward team: for as far as they could tell, this door opened into the interior of a sun.

The door superintendent came over to him. Normanton, Gordey recalled: 47, astrophysicist, married, one daughter, 8, and his wife once held a party card. It was easy to train the memory into becoming a walking card index file. Politicians did it all the time. The one competence of the incompetent, he thought uncharitably: to know whom to tell to do what.

'Nothing new?'

Normanton nodded. 'Nothing at all, sir. It seems we've reached a dead end.'

Sir—the word echoed in Gordey's mind: he was always careful for that respect: only the super competent could afford to dispense with it, and a philosopher, even a slightly mathematical one, was a long way from that in as technological an environment as this. Or was he simply an ordinary egoist? The time was almost come when he could judge for himself.

A dead end, in the centre of a star. The idea made a delayed intrusion on his cheap introspection. There was no sense to it—a graduated test, with no final exam. Having come this far, was it time for the makers of the cylinders to step in?

But he didn't believe that: the makers only acted through their agents, the cylinders. It was an intuition without pretence of proof, but he shared it with almost the entire personnel of the project. There had to be a final test. But what? The ability to exist in the centre of a star? With perfect force shields, it was just conceivable; but to what end? No, it *had* to be the way he had intuited. But he knew it didn't have to be that way at all... Now was simply the time he had to take that chance which was the justification for his rank.

He had forgotten Normanton for a moment. He wondered what emotions had played in his eyes, for the superintendent was looking at him oddly.

'I'll see it,' Gordey said, and Normanton superfluously led the way through the last of the identical chambers.

The door was simply a solid white, of intense brightness, just viewable. Dramatically, it was a let down. But obviously the force screen was programmed so as not to let enough light out to blind: that was the pattern: on your side of any door, you were safe. But the tests had been quite convincing as to what lay on the other sides of doors; and all the indications were that on the other side of this, there was heat so intense that it could only be the centre of a star.

Now!

'A dead end,' Normanton reiterated.

'I hope not,' Gordey said, and flung himself through into the whiteness.

SIR JULIAN WECHSLER fumbled with his shorn hands to unfasten his bow tie as he strode into the main room of his small though sufficiently luxurious London flat. He looked content with the world, as a man should who had just dined rather well with both the Prime Minister and the Secretary of State for Technology, and had been offered, and had accepted, the Under Secretaryship of State at MinTech, with especial responsibility for the project. The fact that a life peerage to get him into Parliament went with the job was a pleasant little bonus.

'Hello, Wechsler.'

In the long silence that followed, Gordey looked Wechsler over. Most traces of the indecisive invalid he had seen in the hospital on New Moon had disappeared; Wechsler had left his chrysalis stage and become fully what he had always been in potential: a politician. But, they had their uses. In fact, they were indispensable.

Oddly, Gordey found himself thinking of those few moments when he had seemed to hang in the flame, wondering whether his gamble that the last door was a test of educated courage had been about to pay off. Wechsler would never have made that jump. But the tests were complex; as well as its technology, they also tested the range of a race.

And the doors had found the Culls wanting.

'What do you want?' Wechsler demanded abruptly.

'There's been some talk,' Gordey began elliptically. 'Talk about not taking a risk with the survival of the human race.'

Wechsler finally managed to divest himself of his bow tie, took a cigar from a box on the table and sat down in the armchair opposite the one Gordey occupied, beside the blazing but simulated fire.

'Just talk,' he said, as he lit up.

'I think not,' Gordey said, 'otherwise I wouldn't be here.'

'I don't believe the British Government's involved.'

'I know that,' Gordey smiled. 'That's what I'm here to complain about.'

'You mean——'

'No. I want that kind of talk stopped. By your government. Incidentally, congratulations.'

Wechsler paused on the edge of thanking him. 'We're not a superpower, and even if we were, we couldn't dictate to sovereign states.'

'Britain had the first fruits of all the project inventions, and has the best force screens in the world, not to mention a fair lead in the New Industrial Revolution. But I won't argue the point. I never expected the British Government to do my work for me. Just to pass on a message.' He paused. 'We finally have matter transmission.'

He watched Wechsler's face, watched him come to full realisation of what that fact meant. The force screens all the nations had built in the last few months, crude though they were, had made nuclear war virtually impossible. You can't bomb through a force shield. But you can transmit through it. The project, with its lower case name, its nine thousand men, its several bases and now its vague affiliation to the UN, was the greatest power on Earth while it kept that secret.

'And we intend to keep our secret,' Gordey said. 'The only technical people who could explain it are two doors away, so snooping will do you no good. And we've arranged things so that any attempt to take over the project, such as would have been necessary to erase the Culls, will fail. Fail disastrously.'

Wechsler had gone white faced with anger. But that was because he was a politician by instinct, and preferred to gloss over the crude wielding of power, disguising it with proper forms. This raw, it grated on him.

'I'll pass the message on,' he said tightly, obviously aware that the message was actually the first assertion of suzerain power over all the nations of Earth that could be made to stick: the beginnings of world government.

Gordey had realised that was the logical consequence of

his actions a long while since. It didn't trouble him; it was inevitable, one way or another. But he also realised that the pill had to be sweetened.

'I'm not making a bid for personal power,' he said. 'I've a story for you as well. One you've heard most of, but missed the end. You see, I also know the precise purpose of the cylinders.'

Stepping quite uninjured on the floor of a cylinder beyond the last, Gordey had felt suddenly elated. He was alive: he had been right. He walked the remaining yards into the open air, without fear. There was no other cylinder, just mountains—and in the far distance, an odd looking mountain hut. He turned about—and saw just mountain rock, no cylinder. Fear caught at his vitals, he couldn't breathe, and then the irregular shadows of the rock sorted themselves out in his mind, and he saw that one of them was really quite regular, the end of the passage. He breathed again, and remembered the hut. This world was still inhabited; it was the end of the line.

But the Culls were not the makers. It had been a long, hard business, discovering the facts about them——

'I know all this,' Wechsler interrupted him impatiently, 'I helped choose the team that analysed their radio transmissions. On the face of it, it's true they don't look like the makers, but——'

'You've seen their technology!'

'They're several generations behind us, and at their rate of progress that could mean a couple of centuries. Their technology would have difficulty duplicating a computer, let alone the cylinders. And there's no sign they've regressed. But——'

'The same "but", and it's a large "but", isn't it? After seeing so many dead worlds, we can't go on appearances; so wipe clean. And after we've done it, they *have* to be the makers, because otherwise it wouldn't have been an act of justice, just murder. And if the makers are dead, the cylinders can no longer harm us. So we can forget them.

'But then, in thirty or forty years, the cylinders will establish a new forward cylinder, on a new living world, and if the occupants of that world fail to get to us and wipe us out in their own well justified fear, the cylinders will leave them for later. And sooner or later, someone will get through, and...'

'How can you be sure?'

Gordey shrugged. 'I can't prove anything, but I tell you it's so, and I was right once before.'

'You were,' Wechsler admitted grudgingly.

'And I've already told you what the cylinders are.'

'A doomsday weapon, cutting a swathe of fear through the galaxy, setting young races at each other's throats...'

Smiling bitterly, Gordey cut him short. 'That's rather too grand.' He paused, then: 'In fact, it's a graded mousetrap.'

Wechsler seemed to crumple back into his chair, as if a sorcerer's needle had been stuck through the heart of his doll.

'It all fits, even to the fastidious detail of letting the various species of mice do the actual killing.' Gordey stopped talking. He could see Wechsler was convinced. There was much more to say, how they could contact the Culls, and use the still primitive matter transmitter to make the leap out into space to contact other races... a federation of mice. The metaphor ought to be ridiculous, but it wasn't.

Or was it? Intelligent mice might avoid a trap, but they don't get down to understanding it, and turning it on its makers.

He wondered briefly about the makers. What kind of race was it that needed so desperately to be alone? Fear of the stranger was a fault; perhaps it could be exploited as such.

Man was a political animal, zoon politikon, and that was his strength, to build upon. A Federation of Not Quite Mice. He almost laughed; he was getting very good at humourless laughing. He would have to remember to play down the mouse metaphor soon: it was strictly shock tactics. Then he remembered he had a question to ask.

'You'll pass the message on?'

For a second time in his life, Wechsler nodded in a particular way.

SPORTING ON APTERYX

by

CHARLES PARTINGTON

Charles Partington, handsome star of a number of famous amateur sf films, has already seen publication in the Arkham House collections of macabre tales, but this is his first appearance with an sf story. New Writings *is constantly promoting new writing talent and in this story of the people of the windy plateau of Apteryx Charles Partington sets up an analogue of a reality we ignore at our peril.*

SPORTING ON APTERYX

NIGHT filled the pre-dawn world with secret places, strange regions where gleaming eyes stared from concealing shadows. Rustlings and furtive movements disturbed the undergrowth and the air vibrated with expectancy.

Minona, moving hesitantly through the hushed fields, stopped and listened every so often to the sound of distant voices, her face taut with growing desperation. Somewhere ahead of her, in the forbidden forest of winds, Mrogre forced his ruined body through trees and tangled bracken, his spoor a dragging trail of blood and angry tears. Between them lay the villagers, shouting, embittered men who drove that which they found hateful before them.

Mrogre was the hunted. Soon, despite his fear, exhaustion would grip his tortured frame. Then he would drop uncaring. Then he would die.

Before Minona lay the forest, a shunned and unknown place where the winds began. Already soft breezes trembled her hair. Behind her the slow gentle bowl of the plateau dipped down towards the village. Ahead, pale moonlight filtered through gnarled fingers of oak and elm. She paused, wondering if she possessed the determination to plunge into that whispering darkness.

Again faint cries of agony drifted towards her on the strengthening night wind. She sobbed, trying desperately to hold back the tears as the harsh teachings of Taltos came echoing into her mind. Minona was only a girl, and the laws of the plateau were without emotion, immutable, hideously unfair. Suddenly she ran blindly into the forest, disregarding the dangers, hoping only to see him once more before he died.

The trees closed about her, shutting off the stars and the lights from the village. With each step the wind grew, moaning in the shadow-held trees. Minona's heart was full of fear and uncertainty. Everyone on the plateau had been instructed from childhood that the forest was evil. It was the place where the winds began. And even worse—beyond the forest lay the edge, the inconceivable end of the world. Minona knew that it was towards this that Mrogre fled.

Sobbing with pity and fear, Minona rushed breathlessly through the darkness, fending off low overhanging branches, her bare feet, accustomed to the open meadows, lacerated and bruised on the rough intertwining roots. The wind howled among the trees, gathering strength, buffeting her slim body with increasing force until it took all her strength to make headway. Instinctively she knew that she was now very near the edge and the old ancestral fears reared unbidden in her confused mind.

Suddenly the forest ended, terminating in a dark expanse of moss-covered stones, across which the wind rushed in demoniacal fury. So strong was that screaming unrelenting wind that Minona was completely unable to make headway against it. Tears of frustration were added to those already streaking her bemused face. She had never imagined the wind could be so strong.

Then far away, on some unimaginable horizon, shadowed peaks burst into liquid fire as the sun rose beyond them, flooding the plateau with light. Half-blinded by tears and the sudden brightness, Minona made out the blurred shapes of men from the village, and beyond, crouching helplessly on the very edge of the world, Mrogre the hunted, staring down into the unknown.

'Avert your eyes!' the sacerdote's thin voice, almost lost in the roar of the wind, screamed a warning. 'Remember the law of the plateau, girl. It is madness to look beyond the world!'

Minona responded unthinkingly, years of conditioning forcing her mind to accept the sacerdote's demands. She dropped into a half-crouch, staring blankly at the mossy stones beneath her feet, thankful to reduce the awful pressure of the wind on her body.

Thinking was now almost impossible. Her mind was in a turmoil. Through half-closed eyes she watched in helpless fascination as the villagers, forbidden to approach the edge, thrust long spears in Mrogre's direction, bone tips quivering in the wind and the dawn light.

The mists were rising now, dense white clouds writhing upwards on the air currents, spilling over the edge of the plateau to be caught and shredded by the ceaseless winds.

Mrogre turned to face the half-circle of spears, his face oddly blank, not twisted with the fear and pain Minona had been dreading. Oh, if only he would look at her! But he seemed oblivious to her presence. For one panic-filled moment Minona thought that the spearmen were going to force Mrogre backwards over the edge. But Taltos the sacerdote was moving among them, shouting instructions in their ears.

If only she could do something! Minona had never felt so helpless in her life. Yet for both their sakes she must not intervene. Whatever happened she had to stay alive. That was what Mrogre wanted.

Now the spear tips touched his body, drawing the skin taut, the men watching for any excuse to plunge the bone barbs into his defenceless flesh. Thongs were produced and thankfully Minona realised that Mrogre was to live, at least for a while longer. She gasped, sagging with relief as the strength left her limbs. Had she not been kneeling, Minona would have collapsed.

Impassive, Mrogre allowed them to secure his tortured limbs. Those chosen by Taltos to fasten the cords carried out the task with obvious distaste, unwilling to come into contact with his tainted flesh. Only when Mrogre was tightly bound and dragged away from the edge, did Taltos approach. Minona saw with horror that the sacerdote carried a long symbol-worked blade. The girl shuddered, trying to prevent a scream, hatred for the sacerdote and concern for Mrogre twisting her senses. As Taltos raised the knife, Minona slumped over in a half-faint, the roar of blood in her ears almost drowning Mrogre's single scream of agony.

When the world steadied and consciousness returned it was all over. Excruciating spasms wracked Mrogre's body. He pawed futilely with bound hands at his blood-filled mouth, strange animal gaspings escaping his throat. With sick despair Minona realised that Taltos had cut Mrogre's tongue out. The sacerdote could allow no word of what lay beyond the edge to reach the village. Despite the danger, the girl was unable to contain a moan of pity. At the sound of it, Taltos looked towards her. He approached, curious, his thin awkward body bent double against the wind, and the expression on his face made her shiver.

'Why did you leave the village, Minona? What impatience overcame your womanly reserve?' The sacerdote's words were like ice in the girl's heart. How wrong she had been to let emotion override her senses. The sacerdote's eyes were hard and unwinking. Minona cowered away from his intense gaze.

'Perhaps you came to see how obscenity is punished?' he whispered, his face inches from hers. 'Do not shudder child, I shall see that this blasphemy does not offend your eyes much longer.' Taltos turned to the spearmen, screaming his commands. 'Take this that was once like us to the village. Hide it away from the sight of men until I decide how best to put an end to its wretched existence.'

Minona stumbled back to the village in a daze. Confused and dispirited, she reached the collection of huts just after midday, and was immediately set upon by several of the older women, who accused her of attempting to avoid her duties. Minona was in no mood to argue with them. Her only thoughts were for Mrogre and how she might possibly be able to help him. Deadly tired, she endured the heavy hands and vicious tongues without complaint, performing her work in a listless fashion which brought more rebuke. Minona couldn't tell if any of them knew of her night-time wanderings in the forest, of actually reaching the edge, but she was conscious of their stares whenever she turned her back on them, and several times she caught whispered conversations about her association with Mrogre.

Towards dusk, when her tasks were finished, Minona was grudgingly given food and goat's milk and allowed to return to her hut. She saw no sign of Mrogre or Taltos on her walk across the village, but she did notice the piles of brushwood heaped upon the open space before the altar. She gazed with a sick feeling at the brushwood, realising that Taltos intended Mrogre should burn before the whole village. What better warning could be given that none who deviated from perfection should be allowed to live? The law insisted that Mrogre, even though he had only recently developed his affliction, should be destroyed. Minona knew that. Once she would have accepted it without a second thought. But how could Taltos justify such a dreadful death?

The girl broke into a clumsy run, tears springing afresh from red eyes where she had imagined no tears were left. In the quiet darkness of her hut she eventually cried herself into an uneasy slumber.

Minona dreamed strange dreams that night. It seemed as if on several occasions before the dawn, Mrogre stood close by her in the hut, looking down, not at her but at some unimaginable place of which she knew nothing. At such moments the air in the little hut swirled and rushed frenziedly as though disturbed by great winds. And with the rushing air came strange and distant voices. Mrogre stood quietly in the midst of all this confusion and the expression on his face caused the girl to whimper in her sleep.

When the first hint of daylight crept across the plateau, Minona left her bed feeling hot and unrested. She stood for a moment in the doorway, staring at the myriad points of light glittering in the greyness overhead, wondering what, if anything, her inexplicable dream had meant.

Out of the half-light came the booming of the great landtoads. Minona shivered at those deep echoing notes. Sonal, the oldest man in the village, claimed he remembered a time when the landtoads were small hopping things no larger than a man's hand. Now they were half as tall as a man and capable of prodigious leaps. Minona recalled Mrogre laughing that they were capable of leaping right off the plateau and back on to it. Though his mouth had smiled she had been aware that his eyes were serious.

Standing there, in the doorway of her little hut, Minona could feel the wind tugging at her hair, watched it rippling through the long grasses. Once as a little girl she had thought deeply about the wind, wondering what would happen if she were to run naked into the forest towards the place where the winds roared. Surely without the weight of her clothes the wind would carry her off, take her far from the plateau to some undreamt-of land inhabited by strange animals? But she had been too afraid to try it. After that, whenever she had to go outside, Minona put on all the clothes she could find, filling the pockets with stones. Only then, though the unaccustomed weight tired her long before her work was finished, did Minona feel safe enough to go outside. For days she felt very guilty about carrying stones around in her pockets until accidentally she discovered that all the other children carried them too. Even the adults, though they would not admit it by carrying stones, constantly affected heavy ornaments or carried accoutrements of iron to weigh them down.

The daylight strengthened and for the first time in her life Minona found herself dreading the dawn. Minona had been subject to the laws of the plateau from birth, accepting them without question as everyone in the village did. Gradually she had learned to reject Taltos' teachings as evil and unnecessary. When Minona had fallen in love with Mrogre, he had displayed no sign of the great mass of flesh which now bulged between his shoulders. Yet even though the weight of that unnatural mass bowed him over and forced him to walk with a stoop, his affliction had done nothing to alter her feelings. Despite the sacerdote's indoctrination, Minona knew that Mrogre was not a thing of evil, that he was still a man and should be given compassion and understanding, not treated as something less than an animal.

Taltos preached the creed of perfection. That to allow abnormalities to flourish unchecked would mean the end of humanity on the plateau and would precipitate the emergence of a sub-species. Look how the crops yielded poorer harvests and the livestock dwindled! Each year it became increasingly harder to sustain life. There must be no lessening of standards, the sacerdote insisted, for this would only result in weakness, in extinction. So every malformed child was destroyed at birth, its body cast over the edge lest its blood contaminate the soil and the crops which sprang from the soil.

For many years Minona had lived by this law without questioning it. Though the doubt had been there before her love for Mrogre, it had been his gentleness that hardened her conviction into certainty.

When the villagers came to collect her, they found Minona huddled in a corner, sobbing bitterly.

The sunlight was harsh after the shadows of the hut. Minona felt rough hands guiding her into the open space before the altar. There, silhouetted against the sky, Mrogre's twisted body hung lashed tightly to a central pale. Sweat and angry weals marked his skin, and his eyes held the vacant expression associated with intense suffering. No flicker of recognition animated his face when Minona was thrust before him.

'Look! Even Minona would not miss the destruction of any who threaten the purity of the race!' The sacerdote's voice carried a vindictive anger which had the crowd surging forward. Minona shrank away from the expressions on those hostile faces. Unmistakably they linked her with Mrogre. Minona knew there and then that she could not hope to escape their hatred.

Taltos approached, his face a mask of religious fanaticism, 'You are all aware of the laws of the plateau!' he screamed at the crowd. 'We must be kept free of all blemished flesh. None must look down into the horror beyond the world. Mrogre has committed sacrilege on both counts. Is there any reason why he should not be cleansed in the purifying flames?'

'No!' thundered the reply. 'Burn him!' they screamed, voices hard with animal passion.

Minona wanted to plead with them to have mercy, to stop; but she was incapable of moving. Fear held her in a paralytic grip from which there was no escape.

Torches blazed into life and at the sight of them the crowd seemed to go mad. Taltos was trembling with passion, his eyes glazed. 'Burn him! Burn him!' he cried, and instantly the spluttering brands were cast on the brushwood, the flames fanned by the gusting wind crackling and spreading rapidly.

'And what of Minona?' The sacerdote's words carried even above the roaring flames. 'Is she free of the stigma of Mrogre's flesh?'

The flames had not yet reached the figure lashed to the stake but even so the crowd was loathe to take its eyes away from its victim.

'Look!' Taltos cried, 'See how Minona has perverted her body with the hunchback's flesh!' Before she could even suspect what Taltos had in mind, the sacerdote grasped her thin shift in both hands tearing it down off her shoulders. Minona stood naked before the hostile eyes of the crowd, a mere girl shivering with embarrassment and fear, her stomach swollen with the unmistakable signs of pregnancy.

Roars of disbelief burst from the men, screams of loathing from the women. Minona carried the hunchback's child. For her transgression against the laws of the plateau she must suffer the same fate.

Their voices were dim echoes in Minona's ears. Only the roaring flames and Mrogre's agonised attempts at screams as the heat began to reach him penetrated her battered senses. She had prayed that she might be allowed to bear his child but even that possibility had been taken from her by the sacerdote's pitiless anger.

'Cast her on to the flames!' came the outraged cry, and instantly it was taken up by the entire crowd. Taltos stood with his arms folded, his eyes blazing. Unable to resist, Minona felt strong hands grip her body, lifting her up, preparing to cast her into the inferno.

The fire was a suffocating wall of tremendous heat. Surely, she thought dimly, the agony of death could not last long? But even before those eager hands could throw her on to the blaze, a dozen voices cried out in surprise, 'Look at the hunchback! Look!'

Minona, gasping in the heat, stared with streaming eyes into the flames. There, where a man died, the flesh around his hump withered and split in that tremendous heat, releasing two white shimmering veils that extended and flexed, firming for a brief instant before charring into blackness and collapsing in ruins around him.

'Wing! Wings!' Came the almost unbelieving cry, 'Mrogre had wings!' Under the sacerdote's insane urgings they had destroyed more than a thing of beauty, they had destroyed a man capable of releasing them from the confines of the plateau. Now he was dead, but the dream was not yet dead with him.

'Minona! Does the girl live?' Eager faces pressed close about her, hope flaring in their eyes as the flames had flared around her lover's body. Carefully they laid her on the smoking grass. Her skin was blackened, her hair almost singed away, and she struggled desperately for air. Water was forced between her gasping lips and she saw with a sudden terrible clarity the question that trembled on every lip but which none dare utter.

A terrible bleakness descended upon Minona as she stared at those silent, concerned faces. Weakly she attempted to struggle to her feet, but the effort was too much. Instantly hands were there to assist her, supporting her without being bidden. From now on they would not be able to do enough for her and her child.

The leaping flames danced in her blank eyes. Tears streaked her blackened cheeks. What other wonders had they destroyed in their fanatical refusal to see the truth, Minona wondered? Now Mrogre was dead and it seemed that all that was worth living for had ended. Racial survival meant nothing to her; for Minona the future had already been destroyed.

Before anyone could prevent her, Minona walked into the flames. Even as the flames roared about her, a smile touched her lips. Though escape by flight had been denied the inhabitants of Apteryx, they might still escape along another evolutionary road. It seemed as if briefly the boomings of the landtoads echoed in her ears...

RAINBOW

by

DAVID S. GARNETT

Uniformed guards, whether of banks, office blocks or old people's homes, are most often regarded as faceless beings. Science had contrived hyperspace and other-dimensional logic to care for the old folk; but when the project was interrupted Lee discovered he had to face up to the emergency, for moral decay operates behind the façade of the face.

RAINBOW

No one knew the exact time when they were cut off. The last people to leave were the half dozen administrative staff members who had to go for a conference. That was a few minutes past ten. A food delivery was due at eleven, but it was usually late.

Several people tried to complain about the lack of electricity, but were unable to because the phones had also become inoperative. The duty portal guards did not notice the failure until past halfway through their shift. 'Half past eleven already,' said Lee, flicking over a page of his magazine.

Looking towards the ten-foot diameter gate, Chris said: 'Late again. Nothing worth eating when we get off.'

'Yesterday's leftovers,' agreed Lee. 'We'd better give Steve and Eugene a call. Make sure they're awake.'

'I'll do it.' Chris pressed a switch beneath the speaker mounted on the wall. He flipped it back into place, then tried another. 'That's odd.'

'What's odd?' said Lee, not even looking up from his magazine.

'There's no hum. It seems broken.'

'That wouldn't surprise me. It's the only thing that hasn't broken yet.'

Chris continued playing with the switches. 'I'll use the one in stores,' he said after a minute.

He was not gone long. 'That's bust, too. The whole works must've gone kaput.'

Lee put down what he was reading and stood up. 'Better report this,' he said. He tried the outside line. It was on a different circuit from the internal network, but it did not work. 'No go,' he told Chris. He turned the knob on the radio and tried the light switch. Neither of them came on.

'Must be a power failure.'

Like everything else the electricity was provided from outside.

'I hope so,' said Lee.

'What else could it be?'

Lee did not answer. He went to the sink, inserted the plug, and turned the single tap full on. It ran for a couple of minutes before suddenly turning into a trickle, a few drops, then nothing at all.

'Chris, I think we're in trouble. Go find the captain.'

Chris looked uneasy. 'Shouldn't we wait till the others get here?'

There were supposed to be two of them at the portal all the time, but Lee judged it no longer mattered. 'No one's going to try and get in,' he said.

'Yeah,' said Chris. 'Yeah.' And he went.

Lee walked up the ramp towards the gate. He stopped two or three yards away. The portal was a huge metal tube jutting a few feet out of the wall. Inside there was nothing but darkness so intense that the eye could not penetrate. It looked the same as it always did. To check if it was working, all he had to do was enter it and walk through to the other side. That was all.

He turned back.

Nine and a half thousand people had no other source of food or heat, light or water. He knew that communication would be restored as soon as possible. But would that be soon enough?

Steve and Eugene arrived before Chris was back. Both had already discovered the telephone and electricity failure.

'I think we've been cut off,' said Lee. 'Chris went to find the captain.'

Steve asked when it had happened, and Lee told them about the administrative staff leaving. They waited in silence, all considering the implications of being alone. Each one knew how tenuous was the link with the other side, but up until now none of them had tried to think about it.

They had pushed it to the back of their minds, pretending it was somehow different.

'I can't find him,' Chris said when he got back.

'Maybe he hasn't returned,' said Steve.

'You mean he left?'

'Rob mentioned he went out last night.'

'Then we're on our own,' said Lee, voicing what they all thought and knew. There was still the possibility that although no one could get in—as evidenced by the lack of deliveries—they could get out. Lee suggested it.

'You're volunteering?' asked Steve.

'I'd go through,' said Eugene, 'but it isn't worth it. Say I make it to the other side, what then? They already know something's wrong and you wouldn't know if I'd succeeded.'

He was right, realised Lee. The only reason he had not thought it through was because he wanted to believe they could get out. Because if he did not believe that, he had no hope. Whatever happens, he said to himself, I'm going to survive.

'But at least you'd be safe,' said Chris to Eugene. He seemed to shiver, and it could not be because he was cold. 'It makes you realise how vulnerable we are. Once they get it fixed, I'm quitting.'

Eugene smiled. 'If they fix it,' he said. 'It is an experiment, remember that. There might be a limit to the duration a portal can operate.'

'No,' Chris said, 'they'll fix it.'

'I agree,' said Lee, although he was not at all sure, 'but the question is: How long will it take? Minutes or days? Or even weeks?'

'We wouldn't last longer than a week,' said Eugene. 'What should we do? Tell everyone?'

'We've got to assume the worst,' said Steve.

'We'd better get the others and hold a war council,' said Eugene. 'We'll have to tell the people something.'

Lee did not say so, and it might have been coincidence that the administrators and the security captain were missing when the portal closed, but he thought they would have to prepare themselves for a long stay here—wherever 'here' was.

Almost the entire population of what was referred to as the 'village' consisted of old people. They no longer worked. They had no reason to leave, and except in rare circumstances were not allowed to. Everything came from outside. They ordered what they wanted, it was delivered and they paid for it. The ten apartment blocks were completely self-catering. They had to look after themselves. The guards were posted at each end of the portal to prevent entrance by unauthorised persons—and there were many who saw the village as an escape route, even though publicity for the experiment and others like it was discouraged.

Lee knew the villagers were nothing but guinea pigs. If this village proved successful, yet others would be established for such people. It was no good housing those who had to keep moving back and forth. The portals were not large enough to move so many. The idea was to get them out of the way and leave more room for everyone else.

After the eight guards had come to an undecision to wait and see, Lee went to the doctor's surgery. There were dozens of 'villagers' waiting in the outer room, and they grew silent and watched him as he entered. He expected to be bombarded with questions; but he was not. They had been given no choice as to where they had been rehoused, and Lee knew they regarded the security men as prison warders. In that, he reflected as he opened the inner door, they were not far from the truth.

'Don't you usually knock?' said the nurse. Her name was Alice and she was the only female younger than sixty in the whole village. She was about half that age. Anywhere else, the man would not have spared her a first glance. She had never spoken to him before and he did not like her tone. 'Can't you see I'm busy?' There was a man sitting on a chair in front of her.

'I wanted the doctor,' said Lee.

'He isn't here.'

'Where is he?'

'I don't know.'

Lee knew. He had gone. That was what he had come to check. Two of the other guards would have been there when he left, but Lee had not asked because he did not want to share his suspicions.

'Why,' she went on, 'has the electricity and water failed?'

'A temporary fault,' Lee told her, his eyes gesturing towards the old man.

She took the hint. 'There's nothing wrong with you. That will be all.' The man stood up and went out. She waited for the guard to speak.

'I think we're cut off. The portal isn't working.'

'You only think?'

'We're not getting anything through. Draw your own conclusion.'

'I'm no expert.'

'Nor am I. I don't think anyone is.' He backed to the door. 'I thought you might like to know.'

'Doctor Whitehead went to visit someone late last night. He said he'd be back around noon.'

'Our captain's gone, too. And the administrative staff.'

'Which leaves . . .?'

'Us, you and around ten thousand others without food or water or . . .' He broke off, shrugging. 'You get the picture?'

'What can be done?'

'By us, nothing. They've got to fix it at the other side.'

'How long will it take?'

Lee shrugged again.

'Thanks for the good news,' she said.

'If you come up with any bright ideas, let us know.'

He left. He supposed something should be done about rationing, but what was there to ration? The water in the pipes would be all gone by now. There were no reserve stocks of food, only what there was in every apartment larder. Lee had not eaten yet and he thought that maybe he should start getting used to eating less. Perhaps there would not be time to starve. How long before the air became unbreathable and they died of asphyxiation?

At the other end of the tube the sun would be at its zenith. But here, where there were only twenty hours, eight minutes and thirty-six point three nine seconds in every day, a sun which was not Earth's fast approached the horizon. Among themselves, they always talked of the strange star as being the sun, and they had no proof that it was not, no matter what they thought. The ones who had measured and analysed it must have known, but their discoveries were not passed down to mere gatekeepers.

We're the ones who live here, thought Lee, but we don't know a thing about it. Did the portal transport them into the past, into the future? The moon was gone and he did not recognise the pattern of the stars, though he had only ever been able to pick out Orion and the Plough. And Jay said the constellations did not belong to the southern hemisphere, either. They could be on a parallel Earth, but the stars did not fit. Perhaps it was a mixture of everything—a different time, another dimension, an alien world swinging about a primary in an unimaginably distant galaxy. Whatever the case, it made no difference to the fact that they were trapped there.

Lee was due for some sleep and at the moment he did not care as much about their predicament as he should. They had been on their own for eight hours. The villagers had been told nothing yet, but it would not be hard for them to realise what was going on. None of them had come to find out. It was as if this only confirmed what they had expected to happen.

'I think,' said Lee to the other seven—he thought Alice might have come but he was wrong—'we should elect a leader.'

'You nominating yourself, Lee?' said Steve.

'Not me. I'll vote for Eugene.'

'Anyone else want to stand?' asked Daren.

Chris looked as though he was about to speak; but he did not.

'Anyone object?' asked Daren.

'Yeah,' said Eugene. 'Me.'

'Too late, Mr. President,' said Steve, 'you're in.'

Daren gave him a mock salute. 'Your orders, sir?'

'Yeah,' said Chris, 'what are we going to do?'

'Talk,' said Eugene.

'Someone should try and get through,' said Rob. 'I know we said it wouldn't do any good; but if someone went through holding a line, perhaps a message could be tied to it and pulled back.' He shrugged his shoulders. 'It's better than doing nothing.'

Eugene nodded. 'Do you want to play Theseus?'

'Tomorrow. If we haven't been rescued. We're not desperate enough yet.'

'Speak for yourself,' said Allan, and a few of them forced a laugh. Anything to relieve the tension. Rob had used the right word: rescued. They could do nothing to help themselves. Going through the gate was the only action they could take, futile though it might be.

'We're in no immediate danger,' said Eugene.

'Face facts, Eugene,' said Jay. 'We're in trouble. Bad trouble.'

'I know that. But it's only a power failure.'

'Long kind of power failure,' said Chris.

'I don't think we'll ever get back,' said Jay. 'This didn't just happen. It was planned. Why isn't the captain here? Why did the doctor and the others leave? So they wouldn't be trapped, that's why.'

'You mean,' said Steve, 'they knew the portal was going to fail and ordered the others out. But why not us?'

'Because we're expendable,' said Jay.

'Why not the nurse?' asked Steve.

'Who'd want to save her?' said Allan, which produced a better laugh than his previous remark.

'Okay,' Eugene said to Jay, 'you think they knew something was going to go wrong and so——'

'No! I'm saying they deliberately cut us off.'

'After all the money and time they've spent on this place?' said Lee. 'All the trouble to build the dome and construct the village simply to sever all links with it? There are cheaper ways of killing off a few thousand pensioners—not to mention a handful of misfits like us.' The fact that the others had left could not easily be dismissed as coincidence, although they all had plausible reasons for going, but it made no sense for them to be deliberately castaway.

'Cheap?' said Chris. 'We'll be dead in a week. Then they can start all over again. They won't have lost the village.'

'It could be part of the experiment,' said Steve.

'To see how we'd react, you mean?' said Eugene.

'Or to see how long we'd live?' said Allan, and nobody laughed this time. 'That's more their sort of experiment.'

'Shut up,' Eugene said, 'all of you. We can't do anything in the dark. We'll carry on tomorrow. Allan, Jay, you're on duty?'

'It's not worth it, is it?' said Allan, but he got no answer.

Lee turned his back on the ten housing blocks. We're not even pretending to care about them, he thought. But should we? Aren't we here to guard them, to protect them?

'Maybe,' he said to Daren, 'we're meant to break through the dome and colonise this world.'

'Could be,' agreed the other, treating the idea as seriously as it had been suggested. 'The eight of us share the nurse—to ensure a mixed gene pool—and eat the rest of them.'

'What we really need is a couple of loaves and five fishes, then we'd be okay.'

'Twice that much,' said Daren. 'And Eugene our miracle worker.'

They were watching as Rob tied a line around his waist and prepared to enter the portal. Two or three of them might have thought he stood a chance, but so far as the others were concerned he was killing himself.

'I feel like a mountaineer,' he said.

'You don't have to go,' Eugene told him.

'I've got nothing better to do. See you later.'

He walked up the ramp and stepped into the shadows and was gone. They only had the length of thin rope to tell them Rob was still moving. The portal was cylindrical with a corridor built through it. The walls of this did not touch the sides of the portal but instead rested on concrete blocks built at either end. A man had to feel his way along to get out; even the brightest light was absorbed in a matter of inches.

He ought to be there by now, thought Lee, and the line became still. Then it dropped. Eugene hauled it back and examined the end of the rope.

'It doesn't prove anything,' he said. 'I can't tell if it's where Rob tied it or if it's been severed.'

'You should have measured it,' said Allan.

'I will if you want to try it.'

Then there were seven, thought Lee.

'Why don't the rest of us go through?' asked Chris.

'No one's stopping you,' said Jay.

'He could have got through.'

No one bothered to comment.

'Now what,' said Jay to Eugene, 'sir?'

'How about leaving the dome?' said Steve, which brought a mixed series of comments in reply to which Steve said: 'There might be something to eat out there. Water. Air. Or it might be a quicker way to die, yes. But we've nothing to lose.'

'Only our lives,' said Allan.

'Listen,' said Jay. He jerked his thumb over his shoulder towards the apartment buildings. 'Why don't we send some of them out and see if they survive? There's no point in risking ourselves.'

'And what do we tell them?' asked Eugene.

Jay patted his holstered revolver.

'We could get them out through the waste chutes,' said Chris.

Waste chutes, repeated Lee silently. A brand new world,

and what do we do with it? Pump out our sewage and rubbish. Probably there were other portals used exclusively to get rid of such inconvenient by-products of civilisation. He had not considered that before. He knew that a few other experimental gates were in operation or being opened. Ones to exploit the resources found, ones to become complete self-contained productive units, and likely ones to be used as prisons. But where were they? On this world? If so, perhaps they could be reached. They would have a route back to Earth. If, of course, their portals had not also failed.

Allan said something about waste chutes being the best place for the villagers, but the most he got was an uneasy smile or two.

'No,' said Eugene, 'We all go out or none.'

'If,' said Lee, 'we found that this world didn't kill us, we could explore it and see if there are any more domes. It would take a while, seeing we'd have to go on foot, but it would pass the time.'

'Pass our lifetimes, you mean,' said Daren.

Nothing else was decided. They simply continued to wait.

They had been waiting a total of twenty-five hours when Eugene visited Lee in his room and said: 'I want to know if I can count on you.'

Lee nodded. 'What for?'

'You, me and Steve to disarm the others before they do something crazy.'

'Daren too?'

'I'm not sure about him.'

'If we exclude him, he'll turn against us.'

'We'll have to risk that.'

'When?'

'Now. Steve's outside.'

'Okay,' said Lee, thinking that if he had refused, he would have lost his gun by this time.

'Thanks, Lee. You can have Alice Tuesdays and Fridays.'

He's only kidding, thought Lee, but how close to the truth was he? He had not seen the woman since yesterday, but he was not the only one who had been thinking of her. One woman and seven men. One day a week each, except that on this world which no one had bothered to name they did not have weeks. But it would not be like that. He, Eugene and Steve would be running the village—until one of them decided to take sole charge. Maybe one of the guards would murder the other six in order to get Alice.

Perhaps, said Lee to himself, I'd better do it before anyone else thinks of it. Winning the nurse was not a very pleasant prospect, but she was better than nothing. Better, anyway, than one of the five thousand grandmothers.

It was a bloodless coup.

After it was over, Eugene said to Steve and Lee: 'I didn't like doing it, but it had to be done.'

Lee wondered if he was right. They had lived and worked together for three (Earth) months. Ever since the dome had been occupied. They were a team, reasonably friendly with each other. But now that was ended forever.

'Do you want our guns as well?' he asked.

'No,' said Eugene. He smiled, trying to make it into a joke, and added: 'Not yet.'

'What are you going to do with the guns?' said Steve.

'I'll handle them.' With that he left.

'Deputy Lee, I think we'd better watch our step.'

'Deputy Steve, I agree with you. Guess I'll mosey along down the saloon.'

Lee found himself walking towards the block which housed the doctor's office, where Alice was. But he saw a uniformed figure crossing over towards the building and go inside. At that distance he could not make out who it was. He turned around and went back. He wondered what happened next.

The long column of people shuffled obediently along the path, up the ramp and into the portal. Some had walking sticks. Others were in wheel-chairs. They talked a little among themselves. Despite their nervousness, on the whole they were pleased to be leaving the village.

The guards stood in two groups and watched them go. One of the group of four occasionally glanced towards the other three, as if wondering if they were going to be made to go through the portal also. The same question was in Lee's mind.

Two of this world's days had elapsed since they had lost contact. Alice reported several people had died for one reason or another and demanded that something be done. Lee had been there when she came to speak to Eugene.

'You've got to do something,' she said.

'All right,' said Eugene. 'We'll send them back through the gate.'

'But it's not working.'

'We can't get anything in, but we can get people out.'

True, thought Lee. The question was: Where did they finish up when they went out? What had happened to Rob? He could have got back safely, they had no way of knowing.

'The sooner the better,' said Alice.

And so it was arranged.

The villagers were told they had to be temporarily evacuated until electricity and everything else was restored. They could take with them only what they could carry. Block by block, they started to leave.

We're murdering them, thought Lee, and they're queuing up to die. Next to him Steve said:

'They might be getting back.'

'Trying to convince yourself?'

'It's better than them dying here,' said Eugene.

'Are you going through?' Lee asked him.

Eugene was saved from having to reply by the arrival of Alice.

'Can I go back now?' she asked.

Eugene hesitated.

Lee said: 'Don't you think you should wait until the others have all gone? In case someone needs treatment.' It's we who need treating, he thought; they're as good as dead already. He tried not to think of them as individuals, as people. Because only when he did so would he comprehend the slaughter in which he was taking part . . . and he hoped he never would.

'I think you should wait,' said Eugene.

'Very well.'

'It'll be about midday tomorrow. We can't get them all through before it grows dark.'

'More are going to die during the night. They'll trip and break their necks, or their hearts will fail, or——'

'I'm sorry,' Eugene said, interrupting. 'I'm doing what I can.'

Lee wondered how she would react when she realised what the security men had done. Perhaps she would not find out, she would walk into the gate not knowing. Would she enter the portal? Would he let her? Lee was determined he would not go through. Inside the apartments he would find enough tinned foods to live on for years. He would rather venture into the unknown beyond the dome than into the other unknown—the portal.

The next day Chris and Jay were missing. The other two claimed no knowledge of their whereabouts. They could have gone through the portal, no one had been guarding it, but it seemed unlikely. It was equally improbable that they had left the dome and gone outside.

'They must be hiding because they think we'll make them go through the gate,' said Eugene. 'We'll deal with them later. Let's finish off the last two buildings.'

'How will you deal with them?' asked Lee. 'Are you going to make them go through?'

'No.'

'Then what?'

'We will all stay here and guard the dome. That's our job.'

'If we don't want to stay?' said Steve.

'No one has to.'

'And Alice?'

'That's up to her.'

'There she is,' said Lee. 'Chris is with her.'

'Chris,' she said when she reached them, 'has told me what's going on. I demand that you stop sending people through the portal. You've no idea what happens to them. They might die.'

'Where's Jay?' Eugene asked Chris.

'Haven't seen him.'

'Steve, Lee, lock these two up. Unless either of you want to take your chance in there.' Eugene pointed towards the gate.

'You mean you're not going to stop?' said Alice.

'I can't stop. If they stay here, they'll die. Through there they might not.'

'But it'll be fixed soon.'

'Three days should have been long enough. Take them away.'

People started going through the portal again.

Alice reappeared as the first group from the final dwelling block began to go through. From nowhere, she was suddenly at the head of the queue of villagers and shouting at them, warning them not to go forward, that if they did so they would die. Lee caught sight of Chris. Jay must have broken the lock to free them.

The people stopped moving forward and the line broke up.

Lee unholstered his revolver. He saw Eugene at the entrance to the portal raise his gun and fire a single shot into the air. He was trying to restore some sort of order, but his action had the opposite effect. He was shouting, attempting to reassure them. Instead, the old people backed away and started to hurry off, returning to their apartments. A man stepped towards Steve, shaking his fist. The guard shot him. Someone screamed and Steve fired again. Lee decided to take his leave. He saw somebody tackle Steve from the rear and take his revolver. It was Jay. He had shed his uniform, putting on ordinary clothing. Jay saw Lee and shot at him.

He missed, then dodged behind a storeroom wall. A mass of people had enveloped Steve's fallen body, and Lee realised there was nothing he could do for him.

He saw Eugene firing into the rioting crowd. He could not see Alice anywhere. Pushing away wrinkled hands which clawed at him, Lee forced his way through the fleeing mob and ran towards the nearest housing block. If he could make it, he would be safe there. It had been the first one evacuated. He reached it safely and waited at the door for a minute, catching his breath and watching the fleeing crowd. A man in uniform was running towards him. It was Allan. Lee kept the revolver in his hand as he slowed and stopped in front of him.

'They might be old,' said Allan, 'but they can move when they have to.'

Lee nodded in agreement. 'I saw Jay jump Steve and take his gun. They got him. You okay?'

'Fine. But they're tearing Daren to pieces.'

'Eugene?'

'I don't know.'

'Alice?'

'I saw Chris pulling her away. What are you going to do?'

'Who knows?' Lee shrugged. 'What about you?'

'I haven't got a gun. And it ain't safe around here. I'll try and bust in Eugene's room tonight and get mine back.'

'And till then?'

'Are you staying in this place?'

'Why?'

'I'll stay with you if it's okay.'

'It isn't.'

'I see.' Allan walked away.

Lee reasoned that he ought to kill him before he became a threat; but he let him go. Then he went to the top floor and chose a room.

There was no reason why the five remaining guards, if there were still five, could not live in harmony. If they united, they could force the remaining villagers through the portal and share what remained—the buildings, the food. They could have two blocks each. Yet Lee knew it was too late for that now; perhaps it had always been too late.

On the top floor alone he had found plenty of food, but his problem was that he had very little to drink. He was trying the floor below when he found Jay waiting for him behind a door. He dropped his gun.

'How did you find me?'

'Allan said you were in this block.'

He should have moved to another. It was stupid to use this one after the other guard had seen him.

'Is Allan with you now?'

'He took a short walk. Through the portal. And that's where you're going. Come on.' He picked up the other gun and they went out of the door and down the stairs.

'I'd rather go outside,' said Lee.

'I'm sure you would. That's where most of the oldsters are.'

'They went out? They survived?'

'Yes.'

'Why not me?'

'I want you out of the way.'

'Because of Alice?'

Jay did not answer.

'Chris and Eugene still around?'

'They won't help you.'

'No.'

They made their way to the exit. Jay kept well back, a gun in each hand, looking around all the time. They reached the ramp. Lee stopped.

'Don't dawdle,' Jay told him. 'I can still shoot you. This way you've got a chance.' He laughed. 'Maybe the ones who've gone through are the lucky ones. The portal might be working in that direction.'

'Thanks for those few kind words.'

'In ten seconds I'm going to empty this in there.' Jay held up the gun in his right hand. 'So get running.'

Lee did as he was told. Perhaps it would be best if he

did go straight through. Even if he stopped just inside the blackness and Jay's bullets missed him, the man would probably wait around to see if he came out. He would not be given a second chance.

The blackness engulfed him. He could almost feel it, it was so tangible. The same moment, almost lost in the all-absorbing dark, he heard a shot. Without thinking, he sent himself diving to the floor. Ten seconds already? He heard two more shots. Jay said he would empty his revolver and had given the impression that the chambers were full. They might not have been, or maybe he had changed his mind, but a few seconds later Lee crawled back towards the entrance and looked out.

Jay was sprawled across the ramp and Eugene was picking up the two guns. Swiftly, Lee backed into the tunnel a couple of feet and stood up. He waited a long time before coming out. His only chance now was to find a gun. Eugene had all three, as well as the four he had taken when the others were disarmed. Lee knew he could wait until night-time and then slip out of the dome, but he would not be safe until the last two were dead.

He should have followed Eugene, but there were all sorts of things in his life he should have done. The other security man had seen Jay make him enter the portal. He did not know he was back in the village, and that was where Lee's advantage lay.

Jay had the right idea in getting rid of his uniform. Lee outfitted himself in a set of clothes he found in one apartment, and took a walking stick from another. He debated whether to make use of a wig he found somewhere else, but decided he need not go that far. A sharpened carving knife provided him with his armament; he fashioned a makeshift sheath and hid the weapon down his left sleeve.

So far as Eugene was concerned, Chris was the only one left. But what of Chris? He would not know how many there were. Did he still have Alice with him? It seemed likely. If Lee was in his position, he would try to get as far away as possible. Jay had said that almost all the villagers had fled the dome, presumably so they would not be forced through the portal. And that was where Chris would have gone. Eugene would have used the same reasoning. All Lee really needed to do was to wait until one of them killed the other—as Eugene had waited to shoot Jay until he had forced Lee into the entrance of the portal.

The village seemed totally deserted as, leaning on his stick, Lee slowly made his way to the dome wall. He had expected that everyone had got out via the waste disposal hatches, but instead he found that a hole had been smashed through the double transparent walls. He could not imagine how that had been done, but he had better things to think about. He stepped out on to the surface of the alien world.

There was no sign of life. Any sort of life. The land was rugged and desolate with very little vegetation, though towards the horizon the slopes seemed far less barren. It did not seem very probable, but that must have been where most of the villagers were hiding. Jay could, however, have been wrong or lying. Most of them could still be within the dome, hidden in their apartments. They were long past the age for clambering over rocks.

Could something have killed them all? Not the atmosphere, because Lee had unknowingly been breathing it since the wall had been breached. Wild animals? Contaminated water? There had to be a reason for the dome's existence. Or was it meant not to keep something out, but to keep the people in?

There were only three people in whom Lee had any interest.

He found Eugene first. It was the noise of a shot which attracted him, the day after he had left the dome. He had soon exhausted all his supplies and had even been forced to drink from a pool of water he came across. As yet, he had felt no ill effects.

When he heard the shot, Lee immediately ducked behind

the nearest outcropping of rock. Eugene—it had to be him —was not far away, and for a short while Lee thought he was the target. But there was no more shooting, and after a few minutes he began to crawl in the direction he guessed the sound had come from.

Eugene was above him, still wearing his uniform, and there was a body a few feet away. It was not Chris's. The guard held a can to his lips and was pouring its contents into his mouth. Lee gathered that he had murdered the man for his food. Yet why had he wasted a bullet? The man would not have been able to get away from him.

Lee became still, waiting. He drew out his knife, transferring the walking stick to his left hand.

Finally Eugene started to move across the rise, and Lee saw why he had been forced to shoot. He moved very slowly and with extreme difficulty, dragging his right leg and putting no weight on it. He kept against a wall of rock, leaning against it and holding himself up with his hands. He was so concerned with not falling that it was easy for Lee to come up behind him and break the walking stick across the back of his head. Eugene fell.

'Are you going to shoot me?' he asked a few minutes later. 'You can hardly make me walk through the portal.'

Lee stood well away from him, checking the three revolvers.

'I could have shot you with Jay, but I didn't.'

Still Lee said nothing.

'I can hardly move. Let me have a gun with one bullet. Put it down there. By the time I reach it you'll be out of the way.'

'Where's Chris?'

'I haven't see him.'

'Alice?'

'No. They must be together.'

'I'd help you to the gate if I had time. I might as well let you have this.' Lee put one of the guns on the ground. 'I'll be listening.' Then he turned and began to climb down.

When he reached the bottom he looked up. Eugene was

leaning over the edge, the gun held in both hands. Lee heard the click as he pulled the trigger.

He began to climb back up. Eugene frantically kept trying to fire the empty gun.

'You shouldn't have tried that,' Lee told him. Then he killed him.

It took much longer to find Chris and Alice, so many days that it seemed he had spent his whole life searching for them. He stayed away from the dome until there were no more old people he could steal food from, whom he could question. Then he returned. He did not even consider the possibility that the portal would ever be reopened. He went into every apartment, ignoring the survivors as though they did not exist. They were simply part of the landscape and there were fewer of them all the time.

If they were outside, they could not remain there forever. He had found nothing to eat, and it would be the same for them. There was very little left even within the village, and Lee took all he could find. He promised to reward anyone who told him where Chris and Alice were hiding, and that was how he found them.

An old woman told him the block, the floor, the apartment. It was one he had checked; he had checked them all. They must have moved in after he had been there. He could not understand why Chris had not tried to kill him. He had purposefully made himself conspicuous in the hope that he would show himself. And when he showed himself he could be killed.

He broke into the apartment at first light. They were both in bed asleep. He had no hesitation this time. He could not risk giving Chris a chance. Lee yanked him out of bed and on to the floor, emptying his revolver into the man's chest.

Only then did Alice awake. She saw Lee. She saw Chris. And she began to cry, sobbing uncontrollably.

Lee sat down next to her and put his arm around her

shoulder. 'It's okay,' he told her. 'You're safe. You're with me now.'

The world outside was safe and inhabitable, and it was up to him and Alice to inhabit it. The few hundred villagers left could be discounted, they would produce no offspring. In ten—Earth—years most would have been dead; here they would last even less.

They were reasonably happy together. Alice never mentioned either Chris or Earth. They discovered hidden stocks of food in many apartments. Some of the villagers, before they died, began to cultivate native crops for food, and these they inherited. Lee even occasionally managed to trap an unwary specimen of a local species of rabbit, and later they had some success in breeding these in captivity. The summers were warm, the winters mild. Lee often thought of how they were like Adam and Eve, though he was careful never to mention this flight of fancy to Alice. The woman once said they had found themselves a private world at the end of the rainbow. The rainbow was the portal.

After two years, when for all their efforts they still had no children, Alice admitted that she had accepted the bounty and been sterilised at puberty. In a way Lee was glad. It felt good to be the only man on the whole planet, on his planet. The only man and the last man. He and Alice would die here, of that he was certain. It was a much more pleasing prospect than the way he would have ended up if he had remained and grown old on Earth. The first, the last, the only. Lee and Alice all alone, at the end of the rainbow.

They were all alone when, forty-nine of their world's years after it had ceased to work, the portal began to operate again.

They were questioned for a long time about what had happened. Lee gave his interrogators an edited version of the truth. He could not understand why he was not believed until one of them told him that so far as they were concerned the portal had been closed for a total time of an hour and a half. And in that hour and a half nobody had either gone in or come out.

So far as the world knew, Lee and Alice were just two more old people. They were moved out and treated the same as any other unmarried seventy year olds. They never saw each other again, or even the world on which they had spent most of their lives. And the domed villages they were sent to were separated by more than mere distance, even though they were half a galaxy apart.

ACCOLADE

by

CHARLES GREY

On any new planet men and women will be concerned with their own fears and desires and here Charles Grey slaps down one more irritation in the way of the universe.

ACCOLADE

HEAVEN waited at Journey's End with each moment bringing unexpected gifts, a shower of novelties to titivate the senses so that they ran from one to the other, voices high in the limpid air, pale faces drawn with excitement as they tried to embrace the plethora of newness, running, examining, turning to look at fresh delights only to be intrigued by something even more wondrous in its implications.

They were children running wild in a brand-new playground filled with entrancing toys and beneath their intoxication at the wealth of strange shapes and intoxicating colours was the greatest intoxication of all; the blood-surging thrill at once again having been given the precious gift of life.

It had been too long, thought Tomlinson, standing in the shadow cast by the great bulk of the vessel, his grey eyes deeply sunken in the dark-ringed sockets of his wasted face. An eternity as they had lain in the artificial wombs doped, frozen, medically dead. A long, long time during which they had shaken hands with eternal darkness and gambled with what remained of their future while around them the ship had gulped interstellar dust and fed it to the ravening heart of the atomic engines from there to be spat in a thrusting tongue of flame. A thrust which had built up a velocity faster than that of light and where were you Einstein? Dreaming in your coffin a universe away? Did the great care if proven wrong?

'John!' Cynthia came towards him, running, breasts loose beneath the thin fabric of her tunic. In her outstretched hand she held a thing of fuzz and brightness, a domed mound of slow pulsation. 'See? It responds to the warmth of my flesh. Life, John! Life!'

Her voice held the mother-hunger of her sex, the need to coddle and cherish, to suckle and to rear.

Quietly he said, 'You shouldn't have touched it, Cynthia. It could be dangerous.'

'This?' She laughed, her voice like bells. 'See how it changes colour as it moves? The way its coat bends as I speak? How could a thing so lovely hold danger?'

He sighed as she held it out to him, conscious of his duty to look and comment and make decisions. But for how much longer? The journey was over; what need now of a captain?

'You are a biologist,' he reminded flatly. 'You know better than to go by appearances. Take it back to where you found it and touch nothing until you are certain it can do no harm.'

'But, John. Really!'

'Do it!' His voice held the harshness of a schoolmaster reprimanding a child. Flushing, she obeyed the note of authority.

Once again he looked at their new world, seeing nothing he had not seen before, the undulating plain covered with tall, branchless trees, the trunks scaled and tapering as they rose, curving gracefully at their summits, moving a little though there was no wind. Above the sky was an incredible blue blotched at the lower horizon by a mass of darkness like a range of distant mountains or an accumulation of sombre cloud. He felt an instinctive dread as he looked at it and yet it was a feeling without reason for it could be nothing more than a natural attribute of this world as was the sun and sky, the plain smooth and pocked with endless declivities filled with water, the trees and, around them, the colourful terrain.

'We can live here, John.' Paul came towards him, thin chest heaving beneath his open shirt, sweat dewing his hollow cheeks. He was thin, like them all, but good food would soon replace the tissue lost on the journey. 'We can cut down the trees and build houses and perhaps use the same material for food and fuel. We can plant crops and use fibre for clothing, seeds for oil, cellulose as a base for plastics. It will mean a lot of hard work but we can do it.

A new world, John. Clean and fresh and ours to do with as we please.'

Again the wild, illogical assumption that there would be no opposition and no danger. Like the others Paul was over-reacting to his rebirth; now that the great hazard was over he assumed that all risk was now a thing of the past.

Children, thought Tomlinson again. We need a death to startle them back into the adults they are. Some danger to manifest itself with screams and blood and broken bones. This world is too soft, too easy. The air, the gravitation, the temperature, all like that of Paradise. We should have landed among snow and ice and bitter winds. Or in a forest inhabited by savage creatures. Man needs the challenge of opposition in order to grow.

Abruptly weary Paul sat at the base of a tree, his figure dwarfed by the vast bulk. A tree, Tomlinson noted, not in the shadow of the vessel, and he wondered if his remaining by his command was a subconscious desire to extend the duration of his authority. While they remained in and close to the vessel he would still be the captain, the father-figure, the voice of authority; but already he felt that the rank conferred by a world which must now be cosmic ash was a matter of habit rather than respect. He moved and sat beside the other man, abruptly conscious of his isolation.

As if at a signal the others came to join them. They were tired, their initial euphoria yielding to a quiet excitement, scientific curiosity finally overcoming childish enthusiasm.

It was a good sign, thought Tomlinson. They would rest for a while and then go into the ship for food and sleep and then, when he had them safely among familiar surroundings, he would subtly re-enforce his command.

'We did it,' said Jerry, lying supine, one hand shielding his eyes from the sun. 'We did what they claimed could never be done.'

'Did we?' Robert sat beside Maria and held her hand as he joined the discussion. 'Einstein said that nothing could travel at the speed of light—let alone faster.'

'The word of one man.' Cynthia sat with her hand on

Frank's shoulder, her head close to his cheek. Already they were pairing off, Tomlinson noted, and wondered which of the remaining women would be his. Peggy? Gay? Lorna? All were young and nubile but one would select Jerry and another Paul and he would have to be content with what was left. And she? Would she be content with the oldest man of them all? A captain without a command?

'The gospel according to Saint Einstein,' said Gay. 'Proved by mathematics and accepted by the faithful. You know, in a manner of speaking, we are heretics.'

'Living proof of the fallacy of a theory,' said Paul. Others joined in.

'A demonstration.'

'A successful experiment.'

'Pioneers smashing obsolete frontiers.'

'The living,' said Jerry, suddenly thoughtful. 'Do you realise that, even if Einstein was only partly right, we are the only human beings alive in the entire universe?'

'The time contraction theory?' Maria shrugged. 'As you approach the speed of light so time slows and, at the critical velocity, it stops. So a journey of several light years at light speed would mean that, on Earth, countless millenia would have passed in relation to those in the vessel.' She shrugged again. 'Once a theory is broken everything goes. We broke it; therefore all the rest is suspect.'

'It was always that,' said Lorna. 'Nothing can travel faster than light because the faster you go the greater your mass becomes until, at light-speed, you would have infinite mass and therefore need infinite force to move it. But what about light itself?'

'An exception,' commented Frank. 'The one which confirms the rule. Light has zero mass when at rest and so could be made to fit the theory.'

'Some theory,' said Frank. 'What about the expanding universe? Distant galaxies recede from us with fantastic velocities. The further we went out the faster they receded until they reached a point where they must have passed light speed. When they did they vanished. Are you going to claim that a galaxy has zero mass?'

'You don't have to convince me,' said Frank. 'You're preaching to the converted.'

'Time,' said Peggy. She had been thinking about what Jerry had said and the concept that they could be the only people alive had disturbed her. 'How long did it take?'

'The journey?' Jerry smiled and moved a little closer. 'Who knows? And by what standards? Ship time? Earth time? Biological time? Everything is relative. A day to us is a lifetime to a mayfly. A two-foot wall over which we can step is an insurmountable mountain to a worm.' He reached out and took Peggy by the hand. 'Enough of discussion. Shall we explore a little?'

'No,' said Tomlinson quickly, and added, for fear they should think him jealous, 'I think it would be best for us all to return to the ship for food and rest. We don't want to overdo things.'

'Hint taken,' said Jerry and rose, Peggy at his side. 'But you're right, Captain. We're all a little bushed, and maybe it would be wise to do as you say.'

Tomlinson could not rest. He rose early and prowled about the vessel as if he were an automaton devoid of free will. The ship was computer-operated, men had no real place in it aside from being passengers and now that it had landed, its work done, the entire mass of cunning fabrication had lost its original purpose and become nothing more than a protective envelope.

However, some instruments had been designed for manual operation and with them he scanned the heavens, brooding over his observations of the sun, his study of the sombre mass of darkness now swollen so as to cover a quarter of the sky. There was something disturbing about it, the hint of a shape impossibly familiar and it worried him. The sun too was unusual, being both impossibly vast and impossibly distant and, as far as he could discover, seeming to be immutable in the sky.

'John?' It was Lorna rubbing sleep from her eyes. Her

hair was dishevelled and her tunic creased but she was warm and human and he responded to her presence. 'I woke,' she said, 'and heard sounds. I wondered who could have caused them.'

Who or what, he thought, but made no comment.

'You look worried, John. Is anything wrong?'

'The sun,' he said. 'It hasn't moved. We landed hours ago, a full day at least, and the sun is still in exactly the same position. And there is this.' He gestured towards the screens which showed the rising shape of darkness. 'What do you make of it?'

'That bank of cloud?' She leaned forward a little, frowning. 'No, it isn't a cloud. It's——' the frown deepened. 'I don't know quite what it is but it seems, somehow, sinister.' Her laugh was strained, metallic. 'Stupid, isn't it? There's nothing on this world which could possibly hurt us.'

'How can you be sure of that?'

She turned at the sharpness of his voice, her eyes searching his face. 'I suppose I can't, really. It's just a feeling I have. It's so warm, so snug and nice outside that the possibility of danger seems inconceivable. And the ship—would it have woken us and released us if there was harm waiting outside?'

She was a child demanding reassurance and yet the demand was justified. The vessel had been programmed to find a safe environment and that is just what it seemed to have done. And yet a machine, like those it carried, could be limited by sensory restrictions. Who could be certain that, during the years of travel, something had not gone wrong?

'John?' She caught his arm. 'Don't look so gloomy. We've a new life to begin and sadness is one of the things we should have left behind. Let's go outside.'

So it was to be Lorna, he thought as she led the way to the port. Not Peggy or Gay but Lorna, not as beautiful as the others, a little older, not so vivacious, but she would do well enough. It was a comfort that at least one problem had been solved.

He felt better outside, away from the enclosing metal,

the machine made by men who could now be only less than dust. The sun still shone warmly from its unchanged position in the sky and a slight breeze stirred the tips of the branchless trees. Like spines, he thought idly as he stared at them and was reminded of something though he couldn't tell what.

He breathed deeply, feeling the lifting of his depression, the unreasonable, illogical dread he had felt while in the vessel. Men were not made to live in a coffin of dead matter fabricated into unnatural shapes. Men were intended to stand with their feet on the soil, the sun warm on shoulders and back, the sound of the wind in their ears. On this world life would be natural and it was a good world, a soft and easy place which they could all enjoy.

He turned and saw the ugly bulk of the ship and the seared place around it where the landing jets had torn and charred the ground. How long? he wondered. They had landed and time would have passed as the ship cooled, more as it woke the passengers, still more as they explored and talked and later slept.

Time which was relative as all things were. A day to a man and a lifetime to a mayfly. Time and size both subject to change. Where had they landed? *On what?*

'John!'

He heard Lorna cry out as darkness fell around them and he looked up and saw the monstrous area of blackness harsh against the sky now blotting out the sun and realised that the thing was growing not because it was getting larger but because it was coming closer, the wind which now whipped the trees coming from the impact of its passage through the air.

And now there could be no doubt as to what it was.

'God!' screamed the woman. 'Dear, God! No!'

And then they ran, but not fast enough to dodge the casual slap which crushed flesh and metal as if it had been the fragile body of some irritating insect.

THE SEED OF EVIL

by

BARRINGTON J. BAYLEY

The Long Golden Afternoon of Homo sapiens *will not suit every person trapped in a culture that denies the chance of immortality on whatever grounds of good taste or civilised behaviour. Time scales stretch in the grand manner in this satisfying story in which Barrington Bayley demonstrates how personal obsession may triumph over apparently insuperable obstacles—but there lies the catch.*

THE SEED OF EVIL

ONE

TIME without end.

Aeternus, being devoid of affective emotions, could not even hate those who had created him; but He knew loneliness. He was a uniquely solitary being who longed for the presence of another besides Himself.

His existence was without end and without beginning. All around him the ceaseless universal vibration of creation and dissolution continued without pause as galaxies were born and died like a whirling mirage of snowflakes. As He gazed down at the never-ending activity, *Aeternus* could see races, empires, worlds, rise up and fall down again into the swallowing void, and He envied the myriad creatures whose lives were given meaning by the fact that those lives must end. His own existence would never end, because He knew both eternity and infinity in which all meaning and pattern disappear.

Aeternus was not material, but was printed into the fabric of space and time, and therefore He could not directly affect anything material, but He could focus His awareness anywhere, even into an atom. And He could *call*, appealing to souls without their knowledge and summoning them to turn unto Him.

He sought some combination of events that would lead a finite being out of the material realm and into the bodiless eternity which now only *Aeternus* inhabited. Only thus could He ever experience the feeling of *other presence* which was all He craved. Surveying the realm of existence, He saw that what was good perished, but that evil outlived all. Therefore *Aeternus* bent his attention to a certain persistent chain of greed and passion, and sent his summons wafting through the waves of creation and dissolution, calling, calling...

Two

THE early twenty-second century greeted the appearance in the Solar System of an extra-solar visitor with little of the amazement or shock that might have been occasioned in the twentieth. The news media gave the event front-page coverage at first, but after a few days relegated it to the back rank of items and concentrated instead on revelations of the following year's fashions. The curiosity of the scientific establishment was, indeed, aroused; but not over-much excitement. The reason for this coolness was partly that it was fashionable, and partly that astronomy, assisted by the advances in space travel that had proceeded unevenly over the last century and a half, had long since revealed that interstellar space contained vast amounts of biochemical material. It seemed inevitable that life must arise wherever conditions were suitable for its reception, and that biology was no more unique to the planet Earth than it was to a Pacific island. With this in mind, the certainty that there would be contact with alien life at some unspecified date in the future had been an accepted fact for a hundred years or more.

Consequently, within two weeks of the alien's having been escorted by a plasma-cruiser to the translunar space station, and from there, after appropriate bacterial investigation, to the sprawling Ignatova Hospital and Research Establishment that lay athwart London's River Thames, the team assigned to study him were already regarding him, most of them at any rate, with equanimity. He was probably an unremarkable specimen, they reasoned, as extra-solar life-forms go.

The one team member who did *not* subscribe to the cult of studied scientific detachment that was so much a part of twenty-second-century life was Julian Ferrg, Surgeon. Julian felt that he had a more intimate connection with the alien than the others, because his scalpels had already explored his body on the operating table. On a day shortly after that event sunlight was filtering pleasantly into a large lounge from a ring of windows set at floor level. Julian's gaze flicked insolently from one team member to another. There was Ralph Reed, the philologist who had already achieved the phenomal task of teaching the alien English; Han Soku, the physicist; Courdon, in Julian's eyes an overly-correct, formal administrator; and Hans Meyer, a cosmologist who hoped to question the visitor on what he called Basic Questions.

Each of them, with the exception of Courdon, was supported by an entire sub-team. Julian himself was assisted by half a dozen specialists in biochemistry, biology and medicine, although the operatons he had performed had been minor: the grafting of an artificial organ to enable the alien to breathe Earth's atmosphere, and the additional grafting of a vibrating membrane to simulate the human voice. Nevertheless the creature had lain at his mercy, its chemical secrets within his grasp. He still thrilled when he thought of that.

For there was one fact about the visitor that they had already learned: he was one million years old.

One million years. The phrase echoed in Julian's mind as he regarded the lounge's sixth occupant: the alien himself.

The closest resemblance to an Earthly creature was probably to a giant turtle, modified somewhat to give an appearance vaguely insect- or crustacean-like. The tall carapace shone dully in the afternoon light. Beneath it could be seen a fringe of hairy legs, mandibles and an occasional glint of metal or some artifact. The newly-acquired gas-sac by which the creature processed air to suit his metabolism bulked somewhat awkwardly to the rear, pulsing gently.

The alien, who claimed to hail originally from the direction of Aldebaran, had explained that his name could be translated as Never Die. It was as Neverdie that they had come to speak of him. Julian simply could not understand why his colleagues accepted this concept with such a lack of excitement.

Neverdie finished a long speech he had been making in cultured, confidential tones that sounded so incongruous coming from his hulking form. There was a long, introspective silence.

At length Courdon said: 'So do we take it that you are asking to be allowed to live permanently on Earth?'

'That is correct, sirs.'

'And what do you offer us in exchange for this privilege?' Julian interrupted harshly. The others glanced at him uneasily. They were all slightly nervous of the lean, angular surgeon and his propensity for breaking out at any time into passionate, arrogant outbursts.

'I offer nothing,' Neverdie replied in the same slow, calm voice. 'As I have just related, I have escaped from a war which is taking place some light years from here. Such is the ferocity of this war that I may be the last specimen of my species left alive. I am here to seek asylum. There will be no repercussions since my presence here is unknown to my enemies. I merely wish to live my life in quiet, at peace on a civilised planet.'

'You flatter us,' Meyer said wryly.

Julian, however, was not satisfied with the alien's answer. 'There is a great deal you could give us in exchange for our hospitality,' he objected. 'For one thing, your spacecraft is capable of fast interstellar travel, a capability we at present do not possess, and it is reasonable of us to expect to be allowed to examine its drive and duplicate it. You may have special knowledge which will help us to advance our technology in other directions, too. And then—most significant of all—is the fact of your virtual immortality. By now you are probably aware that our species has a very brief life-span. It would interest us greatly to know the secrets of your metabolism.'

A mandible clicked before Neverdie replied. 'These matters are a different concern,' the well-modulated voice said regretfully. 'To be frank, I had not intended to be put in the position of striking bargains. My wish is to be adopted as a citizen of this planet, with all the rights of a citizen, including the right to dispose of my assets as I choose. You can appreciate that it is not in my interests to equip your people with the interstellar drive. I chose your planet because it is quiet and little-known.'

Ralph Reed cleared his throat. 'Neverdie's assertions strike me as being entirely reasonable,' he said mildly. 'It would be barbaric of us to accept his presence here only in exchange for tangible rewards like an engine or some other technology. If we are to look at it in terms of gain, it seems to me that merely to have him here is gain enough. Neverdie is a representative of an alien race, an entirely foreign culture, and his presence in our midst will enrich our own culture. Is that not so?'

The others murmured their agreement. Julian flushed angrily. 'This is ridiculous! Have we become so decadent that we no longer see where our advantage lies? It would certainly be——'

Courdon cut him off. 'Now, now, Ferrg, there are procedures for this kind of thing. Let us not forget our manners.' He glanced at Neverdie, embarrassed at the outburst, as were the others. Ferrg had been making something of a pest of himself in the past few days and Courdon was wishing he could have been forewarned about the man. He stood to signify that the interview was at an end.

'Well, Mr. er, Neverdie, the decision does not of course rest with us. It will have to be placed before the appropriate department. However, let me assure you that your application will receive my commendation.'

'I thank you.'

Courdon waited by the door as they filed out. Julian was the last to go. Before he left he glanced back at Neverdie, enraged at his own impotence. That carapaced form contained the most precious jewel in the whole universe, and it looked as though they wouldn't let him get at it.

There'll be a time, he promised himself. *Next time I have him on the table he won't get away so easily.*

Neverdie was glad to be left alone at last. He sank down on his specially constructed divan, relaxed and gave his mind up to sad thoughts.

He thought nostalgically of the other pleasant periods he had spent in the long spell of his existence. Of the fair civilisation beneath the blood-red Arcturus sun where he had recently lived for ten thousand years.

He had told the Earth people something like the truth, but not the whole truth. There had indeed been a ferocious battle from which he had barely escaped. A million years had made him adept at evading the pursuers that sooner or later came at him from all quarters.

But he sensed that at long last he was growing tired. He no longer felt the readiness for endless flight that had once possessed him. He had an intuition, half horrified, half resigned, that this would be his last refuge. Yet while it lasted he believed he would be happy here.

While it lasted ... perhaps that would not be long. Already he scented the beginning of the hunt in the attitude of Julian Ferrg, the jerky one. Unless he acted carefully the surgeon would be drawn relentlessly into the continuing tragedy that was Neverdie's life.

He continued to muse on these thoughts. The sun sank to the horizon, briefly visible through the low windows as a red ball reminiscent of beloved Arcturus. Sleeplessly Neverdie waited in the darkness for it to rise again.

Three

Twenty-second-century London was bowl-shaped.

At the dead centre there still stood, as an archaic reminder, the old Houses of Parliament. Around them the numerous government departments had extended their premises until they swallowed up the previous commercial areas for a considerable distance around, stretching along Tottenham Court Road to the North, along both arms of the river to East and West, and into Waterloo to the South. The buildings were modest in dimensions, however, and mostly of a conservative twentieth-century style. Beyond the centre the suburbs had elevated themselves progressively in a step-like version of the *habitat* mode, rising at the perimeter to just under a mile in height. At close quarters the *habitat* suburbs, with their lack of any clear linear organisation, were like a three-dimensional jungle—especially since Londoners had rediscovered the pleasure of gardens. From a distance they merged into a sparkling, curved surface and gave the city the impression of being a vast arena. When the sun rose over the edge of the perimeter, the great bowl acted as a sun-trap; when it fell below it, illumination continued to filter through the myriad interstices and filled the interior with a panorama of light and shade.

Julian's airplat floated down into the bowl, mingling with the traffic that hovered over the city like a haze of gnats, and came to rest on a rooftop platform. Courdon's office was in Centre Point, a twentieth-century structure huddled among other, more modern buildings. Julian passed through the rooftop reception hall to the administrator's office.

Courdon was waiting for him. He greeted Julian coolly.

'I think I know what you're going to ask me, and I fear you will be disappointed,' the civil servant began.

Julian strode energetically to the proferred chair and flung himself into it. He looked quizzically at Courdon.

'Well?'

'Neverdie has been granted the world's first extrasolar immigration permit. In five years' time, if all goes well, he will be given west-European citizenship. To state things from your point of view, the permit was given with no strings attached. And Neverdie has declined to discuss the matter of technological advancement.'

'You've approached him about the question of longevity?'

'I conveyed your request to him, yes, but he's not willing to co-operate. He hinted that knowledge of biological permanence, to use his term, would not be to our benefit.'

Julian's lips compressed in annoyance. 'Really, I can't understand the attitude of you government people. Whose planet is this, ours or his? And what about his ship? It should be impounded.'

'But why? It's his property. We must live according to the law.'

'The law! The law is whatever it's made to be. Who can Neverdie call on to back his case? Nobody; he only has our gratuitous compliance. Anyway, the ship isn't important. Immortality is, and that's what we have to think about.'

'I'm not sure I agree with you. I think Neverdie's right. Immortality would be a disaster for us. Everything we have is built around our present life-span and, speaking personally, I'm quite satisfied with it.'

'You would be,' Julian grunted. 'But never mind about that, not everybody in this world is so complacent. Surely there's some way we can get it out of him? How does he propose to live? Or is the government taking care of that, too?'

'As a matter of fact, no. Help was offered, but Neverdie refused it. He proposes to earn money by writing books and giving interviews. I believe he is buying a house in St. John's Wood.'

The surgeon meditated sombrely. 'I'll tell you what I think,' he said. 'This citizenship business is all nonsense. Dammit, you're treating him just like a human being! He isn't. He's a creature from space. If he won't tell us what we want to know, we should take it from him by force, by physical examination. Just give me a few weeks with that body of his and I'll find out everything.'

He did not see fit to mention one likely possibility—that Neverdie probably did not know himself what kept him alive, just as the average person could not describe the processes of his own metabolism. Neither did he mention that the examination he suggested would almost certainly prove deeply injurious to the subject. Courdon, however, was outraged that Julian should suggest it at all.

'Really, Ferrg, you forget yourself! We couldn't possibly

consider such an action! What would the rest of the world say? For that matter, what would Bonn say?'

Julian waved his hand, impatient that the perpetual tussles between London and Bonn, twin capitals of West-Europe, should be brought into it. 'There was a time when progress was thought to be important,' he said. 'Now we have an unprecedented opportunity to increase our knowledge and nobody is remotely interested.'

'Times change.' To Julian, Courdon looked infuriatingly smug. 'The world has settled down now. There is planet-wide agreement on all basic issues. The problem of material wealth has reached an equitable solution. Why should we strive after distant dreams any more? Life is pleasant, why not enjoy it?'

Julian knew all about the philosophy of the Long Golden Afternoon of civilisation that was so much put about. As far as he was concerned the Long Golden Afternoon was one long bore. He felt stuffed to his ears with it. He would sooner have lived in a previous age when action counted for something and the law was an obstacle men would contemplate breaking if the returns were big enough.

In this case they were big enough.

He rose to his feet. 'Nothing lasts forever. The times will change again. And that creature will have to watch out for himself.'

Courdon merely stared at his desk as Julian strode from the room.

In the evening Julian's airplat took him to the South tiers of the London Conurbation. He parked in a garage five hundred feet above ground level and entered the adjoining apartments.

The people gathered there were all either close friends or sufficiently in sympathy with Julian's private philosophy to be trusted. They formed a tightly knit in-group jarringly at odds with the normal standards of the time. And they all, to one degree or another, wanted to live for ever.

They listened to his account of the meeting with Courdon with an air of cynical acceptance. They knew it already.

'Decadent and cowardly,' said David Aul. 'Still, that's life.'

Julian gulped wine from a huge goblet. 'We'll take it into our own hands.'

'*Mon Dieu*, that's going a bit far, isn't it?' said another voice.

'We've already discussed it.'

'Yes, but were we serious?'

'Of course we were serious, you damn fool!' Julian's eyes flashed angrily at the speaker. It was André, a vague, unpredictable Frenchman. 'Do you think I waste my time on daydreams?'

André shrugged.

'Anybody who has no stomach for it, walk out of here right now,' Julian demanded. 'If you want to squeal on us, go ahead and do it. We'll simply deny everything and that will be that.' *And then we'll do it anyway a few years later*, Julian thought to himself.

He didn't wait for answers but snatched up a bottle of wine and retreated to the corner of the room where he flung himself on a couch and continued to drink swiftly and heavily.

Ursula Gail detached herself from the group and smiled down at him with clear hazel eyes.

'So you're really going to do it?' she said, speaking with a slight German accent.

'Naturally.' Seizing her wrist, he pulled her down on the couch with him.

'But what about the risk? Somebody might betray us. What about me? Suppose I do?'

'If you do I'll kill you.'

She chuckled softly, leaning close and nuzzling his cheek. 'That's what I like about you, Julian. You're so *wicked*. I don't think there's one good impulse in you.'

'What is good perishes; evil endures.' He shook his head,

momentarily confused. What had made him say that? He was already slightly drunk.

She noticed his unsteady movements as he scanned the room for another bottle. 'Aren't you drinking too much? I thought you were operating early tomorrow morning.'

'What difference does it make? These days all the instruments are electronically controlled. I often operate dead drunk. Never lost a patient yet.'

The drink and the music that came from a small player were making him feel warm and mellow. He had a pleasant feeling of anticipation, of a decision made and of having burned his boats behind him. The others were almost certain to back him. What was there to lose? Liberty? Life? They would be lost anyway, in a few decades. Against that was balanced the possibility of life eternal.

The final plans were already vaguely foreshadowed in his mind. It could not be done for a few years yet. The present time was too soon, and besides there was much preparation to be completed. A ship would be best, he told himself. A yacht fitted with everything they needed and in which they could sail the oceans while completing the work, safe from detection.

Afterwards came the question of whether the alien's method of immortality could be adapted to a human being. They all knew that the probability of that was rather low. But then, who but a desperado ever commits himself to a philosophy of action, not to say of crime? Julian's mouth twisted sardonically as he contemplated the thought.

A short while later he took Ursula into an adjoining bedroom. Breathing lightly in the darkness, she suddenly spoke.

'What would you give up for immortality, Julian? Would you give up this?'

'I would give up everything,' he said. She asked no further questions. They both lay staring up at the darkened ceiling, imagining a future without end.

Four

FIVE years passed before Julian deemed the time was ripe.

Neverdie had settled quite well into human society. He was only occasionally mentioned in the mass media now and lived the life of a near-recluse in a large house whose interior had been restyled in the Georgian mode—a fashion the alien seemed to prefer to all others. His needs were financed out of the returns from his books. Julian had studied them all assiduously, especially the lengthy *Aldebaranian Social Organisation*, but had learned nothing useful. He was not interested in how an extinct species formed 'hedonistic rank-order', as was apparently the case. Neverdie had also written a number of competent but off-beat science fiction novels with some interesting details, but nothing touching on biochemistry.

On the evening of the 18th July, 2109, Julian and his comrades struck. An airplat glinted in and out of light and shade in the approaches to the Northern suburbs and entered the habitat jungle.

Julian was flying, with four others in the seats behind him. The airplat drifted through the three-dimensional maze, surrounded on all sides by lavishly decorated walls, windows, doors and ceilings and the gardens that hung profusely from almost every roof. After a short while they arrived at Neverdie's dwelling.

Although lights shone already from most of the surrounding windows, Neverdie's house was in darkness. Julian parked the airplat on the flat, bare roof, close to the roof door. He got out, stepped to the door and tested it. The door was unlocked.

He had previously had the house cased for alarms in the guise of a magazine interview. Apparently, there was none, which to Julian's mind was an extraordinary oversight. He beckoned to the others. They padded after him and the group descended into the dim interior.

Julian paused briefly to enjoy the elegance of the rooms. Neverdie certainly had good taste. But for the strangeness of the furniture, which was built to serve his form and not the human, this could have been the home of a cultured, educated Englishman.

They found the alien in the downstairs drawing room, apparently asleep. Julian knew that he would sometimes sleep for a week without waking. He drew a small cylinder from his pocket, releasing from it an invisible gas. To the humans in the room it did nothing; in the Aldebaranian, however, it induced a deep unconsciousness. Neverdie would not wake now.

Julian had learned that trick in the course of his previous medical attendance on Neverdie. They lifted the body on to a stretcher; it was surprisingly light.

Back at the roof door Julian glanced quickly around. He did not think they were observed. Impatiently he waved the team on. In seconds their cargo was safely aboard the airplat.

Nosing out of the habitat region, they flashed into the open air again, and went planing Southwards.

At almost the same time Courdon received a call.

Five years ago, sensitive to Julian's purposefulness, he had taken precautions. Neverdie's dwelling was bugged.

After all this time the surveillance service was slow to respond to the announcement that uninvited persons were present in the apartments. Following a procedure already laid down, their first move was to contact the administrator.

In his own home, Courdon took the news with astonishment and, at first, disbelief.

'Can you give me a picture of them?'

The surveillance operator spoke calmly. 'They have already left the house. We are tracking them in an airplat, flying towards Greenwich. We can pick them up at any time you like.'

'No, not yet. If they have the nerve to kidnap Neverdie then this is a planned conspiracy. Let's wait to see where they lead us.'

The kidnap party disappeared into the ascending tiers on the South side of the city. Police plats, nosing like fish in an undersea coral bed, cruised after them at a calculated distance.

In the interlocking complexity they soon lost their quarry, but were not worried. In the next few minutes they would find it again, probably at its destination.

And so they did. But in those few minutes they were already too late. They found the airplat, as well as the house where it was parked, deserted. Their reaction was to search the neighbouring buildings and to think in terms of a switch to another airplat. It did not occur to them until some time later to think of an ocean-boat mingling with the river traffic beneath their feet and heading rapidly into the open sea.

Watching from his home, Courdon cursed.

In the Mediterranean, aboard the plano yacht *Rudi Deutschke,* Julian faced a vacillating situation.

In short, his colleagues had got cold feet.

'C'est dangereuse, mon ami,' André said glumly. 'By now they will be looking for him. What if they should guess he is at sea?'

'How would they guess, you fool?' Julian retorted. 'They might think of it as a remote possibility, that's all. And as for a sea search—well, have you any idea just how many ships are on the oceans at any one time? Damn near a million, I should think.'

'Just the same,' David Aul put in carefully, 'we won't be safe until that creature below decks is washed over the side, or what will be left of him. How long is all this going to take?'

'It will take months at the very least, so stop panicking. And you're *never* going to be safe, get that through your head. And for God's sake try to work up a little backbone!'

I'll ditch this lot as soon as it's convenient, he told himself. *When it comes to it they're nothing but a bunch of nuts who get jittery the moment their fantasies start to turn into reality. Except Ursula, no sense in wasting her. She's got more guts than the rest of them put together. Funny thing about some of these women.*

Actually the research to be done on Neverdie was only the first stage. Then would come the problem of learning how to apply the knowledge gained. That would almost certainly take years.

His plan was to pass through the Suez Canal and into the Indian Ocean, where West-European influence was slight and the chances of their being apprehended correspondingly reduced. Once they were finished with Neverdie he would switch to the land for the longer stages of the work. India was a delightfully corrupt place and he knew where he could be kept indefinitely from view of the law, with full research facilities, until this programme was complete.

When he felt he was sufficiently rested Julian began.

Taking with him David Aul, who was a trained biochemist, he descended to the space amidships that had been equipped to fulfil all the functions he thought would be necessary.

There was enough here to take the alien apart muscle by muscle, nerve by nerve and molecule by molecule.

They both stared at Neverdie as he lay strapped to the operating table. Surrounding him were the electronic pantos that would do all the cutting and manipulating—Julian didn't trust this job to manual dexterity, and besides he would be working at the cellular and molecular levels. One half of the working area was devoted to biochemical analysis and the mapping of the nervous system. If they found that they needed any extra equipment, Julian was confident that they could get it in India.

'What if it's something that we *can't* find out?' Aul commented.

'I don't think it will be. I'm more than half certain that Neverdie's immortality isn't natural to his species. That just wouldn't make sense, would it? Any biological organism has to die, otherwise the ecology it lives in couldn't work. I think he acquired everlasting life by artificial means and if that's the case then we should be able to find out how.'

Julian flicked a switch and brought the hum of power to the workroom. 'To begin with, let's see if our friend has had a change of heart that would make all our work unnecessary.'

Using a dropper, he administered a few cc's of a pungent-smelling liquid to an organ just beneath Neverdie's carapace. The alien, who was strapped upside down to reveal a mass of appendages, opened milky translucent eyes and stirred feebly.

The eyes swivelled and focused on Julian. 'You are making a mistake . . .' the voice diaphragm said weakly.

'It's *you* who has made the mistake,' Julian said. 'You know what we want: give it and we'll spare you.'

'No . . . I cannot.'

Julian paused. 'I would like to put a few questions to you,' he said finally. 'Are you willing to answer?'

'Yes.'

'Firstly, is the secret of immortality something I could find? I mean, is it an analysable property of your body?'

'Yes.'

'Could it be applied to myself?'

'Yes, more easily than you think.'

Julian's excitement mounted. 'Well what is it? If you'll tell me this much, why won't you tell me the whole thing?'

Neverdie squirmed. 'I beg you, do not seek immortality. Forget your lust, leave me in peace . . .'

'I've got to!' Julian exclaimed in sudden inspiration. 'It concerns some specific substance, or something, that your body contains, doesn't it? To have it myself I'd have to take it away from you, wouldn't I?'

Suddenly Neverdie became still, as if in despair. 'Your guess is close. But you must abandon your intentions. You do not understand. This is your last chance to leave well alone.'

'I understand that you're trying to save your own skin. Unfortunately in this universe any item in short supply goes to the strongest party.' He glanced at Aul. 'Don't say anything of this to the others. We have to get in all the facts before revealing anything that might cause trouble.'

Aul nodded, his face clouded.

'Then let's get to work. Good night, Neverdie. The curtain is falling.'

From a nearby nozzle he released more of the gas that to the alien was an instant general anaesthetic. Neverdie's appendages twitched once. Then he was still again.

They were sailing past the Gulf of Akaba when Courdon finally caught up with them.

Since losing track of the quarry in London, he had frantically been trying to identify and search all vessels that had travelled down the Thames in the following two days. The number ran into thousands. There was nothing to connect the *Rudi Deutschke* to Julian Ferrg, and it was with great difficulty that he managed to persuade an Israeli coastal patrol to make what was strictly speaking an illegal search.

At the time Julian's investigations had only reached a rudimentary stage concerned with biochemical analysis using tissue samples sliced from the alien's inert body. Neverdie was very lucky: no real damage had been done.

So engrossed were Julian and David in their work that they failed to hear the whistle of the patrol craft as it flew overhead. Julian merely looked up with a frown of annoyance as he heard shouting from the deck above, especially the shrill voice of Ursula.

'Get up there and tell them to stop their damned row, David,' he ordered angrily. 'I'll have no arguments on this junket.'

Aul moved to obey. But at that moment the door flew open and the bereted coastguards stood framed there. For long moments they stood, staring at the scene, their tanned faces turning pale.

'What do you want?' Julian shouted in an enraged

voice. 'Get out of here, damn you! Can't you see we're busy?'

The guards unshouldered their arms. The game was up.

At his trial Julian fell back on the perennial refuge of the scoundrel: patriotism.

He had done it all, not for himself, but for humanity. 'Even when governments are soft,' he said, 'there are some who believe that mankind must advance by whatever means possible. My work, had it been allowed to continue, would have brought incalculable benefits to this planet.'

The audacity of his statements probably did serve to soften his sentence, as had been his intention. His companions were given ten years apiece in a corrective institution. Julian, as the ringleader, was sentenced to fifteen years.

Five

On his release, fifteen years later, Julian was forced to make a drastic reappraisal of his position. He was no longer a young man in his early thirties: he was forty-eight. Although he had kept himself fit during his imprisonment and was still lean and active, the sands were running out.

Neither could he hope to repeat the escapade of fifteen years previously. Struggling in his mind was the small thought that his whole venture was madness and that he should return to a normal life, or what was left of it. But the thought, which at an earlier stage in his life would have seemed sensible, quickly died. The coming of Neverdie, he realised, had wrought a transformation in him and the pursuits which once appeared worth while now seemed pale and futile. Only one thing was of obsessive importance: to attain the lasting life besides which the present life was but a shadow.

Swimming in impudence, Julian even managed to obtain a final interview with Neverdie. In truth it was a desultory move, a last attempt to gain the alien's co-operation.

The interview was held in a somewhat strained atmosphere, not because of any feelings held either by Neverdie or by Julian, but because also present were Courdon, the philologist Ralph Reed and two policemen. They bristled with hostility, a mood which Julian could endure without the slightest discomfort.

'You know why I'm here,' Julian said. 'I've come to ask you once again to give the secret of your long life to humanity.'

'Humanity does not want it. Only you want it,' Neverdie observed.

'Not only me. There are others. How long do you think you can keep it to yourself? At the moment society protects you. But societies change. Don't you know what risks you run, what danger you will have to fear from men in the future? Why not at least give us the information, even if you can't give us the means. We might find a way of duplicating the special substance, or biological arrangement, of whatever it is that keeps you alive. That way you'll save yourself from persecution in future centuries.'

'I shall take my chance,' Neverdie told him in a studiedly neutral tone. 'Luckily, beings as ruthless and determined as yourself are rare.'

'Rare, but they exist!' Julian rasped in an outburst of temper. He jumped to his feet, suddenly aware of how Neverdie saw him: as a mayfly, an insignificant, brief creature whom the alien was patiently waiting to see die. It made him feel foolish and despicable.

'You overgrown beetle, one of us will get you!'

Abruptly, he left. Ralph Reed let out a sigh of relief. 'What an extraordinary fellow! It's almost incredible that a surgeon should be so ... well, evil. And yet he's brilliant. They say he's saved thousands of lives.'

Throughout the interview Courdon had calmly smoked a pipe. He puffed on it, thinking. 'Ferrg admits that he doesn't think of Neverdie as a person—with respect to yourself, Neverdie—and he tries to justify himself that way. But I don't think he thought of all those whose lives he saved as human, either. Human beings don't exist for him. They're just objects to be experimented on.'

'A lot of people think that way, especially in experimental science. But they're not like Ferrg.'

'No, he's different. It's not scientific objectivity with him. It's something else. Something completely, utterly selfish.'

Outside, as Julian walked towards his airplat, he encountered Ursula Gail.

'I followed you here,' she told him with a knowing smile. 'I was curious. What are you planning now?'

'Nothing. To interest you, anyway.'

She pointed to an inn that lay at the bottom of a long, wide, curving sweep of steps. 'Come on, let me buy you a drink.'

He allowed her to lead him into the inn. Uneasily he settled with her in a corner, a bottle of white wine before them.

He looked at her. Fifteen years didn't do much to improve any woman. But she still looked fairly young and she was still beautiful in her particularly exciting kind of way.

'So you're really not planning another snatch?'

'No.'

'Or a deal with Neverdie?'

'There's no deal. That's what I was there about.'

She gave a low, regretful laugh. 'Don't worry, I wouldn't want to be in on any more mad schemes. The others feel the same way too. But unlike them I don't feel bitter about what you got me into. What's the use?' She tilted her glass. 'As a matter of fact I was looking forward to seeing you. I thought we might——'

She glanced at him familiarly with the same bright, hazel eyes he had known before. Hastily Julian looked away. He pushed himself from the table and stood up.

'Sorry, Ursula, time's too short. Finish the wine yourself.'

Without looking back he strode out.

One phrase that Julian had used to Neverdie was the kingpin of his strategy.

Societies change. He had already messed up one opportunity. To gain another he had only to forward himself some centuries into the future.

The technique of putting the human body into suspended animation, permanently if need be, was already perfected. It was practised on thousands of people with incurable diseases who hoped they could be cured when they awoke. Once initiated, the process required no expenditure of power and assured Julian of personal, self-dependent survival.

He sank most of his assets, which were large, into the time-travelling chamber. He was prepared, if necessary, to pursue Neverdie down the millennia.

There was one risk, of course. The Government, with what struck Julian as insane complacency, instead of impounding the alien's tiny interstellar ship and extracting from it the technology to take mankind to the galaxy, had merely allowed him to store it in a garage beneath his house. It was conceivable that Neverdie would leave Earth before Julian awoke. But he did not think so: the Aldebaranian seemed quite settled, and if what he wrote in books was true there were not too many places he could go.

With this point in mind, however, Julian pursued his plans in utmost secrecy. His time-vault had two compartments: the suspension chamber which could also serve as living accommodation, and a larger chamber which was virtually a duplicate, except that it was even more elaborate, of what had been aboard the *Rudi Deutschke*. The vault was of the most durable construction. It could not rust, corrode or weather. It was built of the new type of carbon-bonded material that had properties close to that of diamond but which was too expensive as well as too long-lasting for use in normal construction.

The basic timing mechanisms were of the same material. Julian had made an arrangement which was as close to immortality as Earthly technology could make it. The vault and most of its contents—including many of his surgeon's instruments—would persist and be functional even when London itself had crumbled and vanished. Not that he anticipated such a long tour of duty. He set the timing mechanism in the first instance at five hundred years hence, knowing that in that period even the noblest societies could turn into the most debased.

The centuries passed. The society of West-Europe underwent a number of vagaries, most of which Neverdie predicted and accommodated himself to fairly well. He became an obscure but permanent, little-noticed resident of London. It was an extraordinary fact about the human species (Neverdie had observed it was a fact about most species), that in spite of its avowed interest in the universe at large in the long run it was interested only in its internal affairs. Neverdie was expert at staying out of the way of those affairs.

But in one important respect Julian had underestimated him, just as he had underestimated Courdon. Neverdie was watchful. He took care to get news of Julian. When that news suddenly stopped he engaged agents to get news of him from wherever in the world he might have moved to. But no news came; Julian Ferrg had disappeared.

Neverdie was a careful being who moved slowly. His great advantage over all his enemies was that he had more time than they did. And in his chequered career he had met the suspended animation ploy before. This, in his opinion, was what Julian had done.

Locating the surgeon's time-vault was not a matter of urgency. Neverdie did it without making any overt enquiries. He merely collected a large number of insignificant facts over a long period of time and watched the rebuilding pattern of London over the decades. His intuition that the vault was in London was fairly quickly confirmed; and some detective work concerning the legal arrangements of several possible sites told him, roughly one hundred years after Julian's internment, exactly where the surgeon was.

One night a twenty-third-century-style airplat drifted into the ancient, semi-underground part of the city. The lighting system was poor in this quarter and it glinted palely over the outlines of the vehicle. At length the airplat ventured up a dusty alley and came to rest before a decaying building beneath a warehouse.

Neverdie crept from the airplat. In his manipulatory limbs he carried a number of tools of a type which Earth did not have. Plastic and masonry gave way to make a small hole, like an enlarged rat-hole, through which he could crawl.

The interior was pitch-black and oddly cold. With a click Neverdie brought to the scene a dim light by which a human being would scarcely have been able to see at all. In the depths of the run-down building he eventually discovered the smooth, cold exterior of the vault.

Neverdie switched on the other cutting tool he carried. Its slim beam did not even carry enough energy to light a match, yet it neatly disassociated the bondings of the material and carved out a neat section. Inside, Neverdie found Julian pale and dead inside a cylinder of the inert gas argon.

The Aldebaranian was not a murderer. His actions were preventive, not assaultive. He found the timing mechanism and after a minute's study disconnected it, leaving the reviving device inactive. Julian's suspension would never end now without outside aid. Satisfied with his work, Neverdie repaired the incision in the wall of the vault, cleared up the other evidence of his intrusion and left.

Six

London crumbled and rose again. Millennia passed and even geography changed, but always a city stood where London had been, except for one period when it was replaced by a lake. And in all this time Neverdie continued to dwell on the fringe of human society, building for himself the image of the perpetual hermit, the Wise Being on the

Hill, the Oracle, anything that would protect him from superstitious vindictiveness.

There were many occasions when Julian's time-vault came under scrutiny during the periodic rebuildings of the city. Each time when it seemed likely that the vault would be opened (and the waxing and waning technology did not always make this possible) Neverdie would intercede and persuade the authorities to leave it untouched. Under his auspices it was eventually removed to a site on a hill overlooking the city to the North.

But at last the age of *Homo sapiens* itself passed.

For a long time Neverdie had seen the end coming, but he had offered no hint of it to his long-standing hosts. Human scientists had never quite understood the laws of evolution. They had not realised that just as an individual animal had a natural life-span, so an entire species had a natural life-span which was predetermined by its hereditary genes. Nature, having made one dominant species, liked to wash it down the drain and try something different with another. For this reason evolutionary changes sometimes proceeded with suddenness. *Homo sapiens* had emerged from primate stock over a span of tens of thousands, rather than of millions, of years, and the death of the species was coming just as suddenly as had the birth. With the running down of the genetic clock births became fewer, society collapsed and the vitality of the human race entirely vanished.

Even while the last remaining men died nature was already preparing their successor: *Lupus sapiens*, the intelligent wolf.

In a crude hut some miles from the ruins Neverdie finished his long period of meditation. He had reached a conclusion: his host species was gone, and the arising of the new dominant species would be a turbulent period in which it woud be hard to survive; therefore, the time had come to be moving on.

As he roused himself his artificial voice-diaphragm whispered rustily. It was nearly four thousand years since its last replacement and the thing was rotting. He would discard it soon, when he could find the time.

He lifted the door-latch. The wooden door creaked open, letting in a cold draught of air. He crept out on to the wilderness of the moor and set out for the ruins, keeping a wary watch for any predatory wolves. He lived in a state of armed truce with them, but he knew that they were liable at any time to renew their attacks on him.

He reached the ruins without mishap. They were little changed from when he had last visited them, except that the wolves had begun to tear down the brickwork to fortify their camps. They had not yet learned to work metal, however, and the vault containing his starship was intact, though it did bear the marks of their rude tools. It looked incongruously neat amid this fallen tangle of stone, a perfect dome washed clean by the rain. The lock grated reluctantly as he made his entrance, and in the dim light within Neverdie set to work to prepare the vessel for flight.

The starship had benefited from his servicing it every few centuries and was still in fairly good condition despite the difficulty of replacing some of its components (there were some materials that could not be obtained in the Solar System at all). Within three days he deemed the vessel fit for interstellar flight, or as fit as it was ever likely to be. Now all that remained was to prepare a route from his maps: the work of hours. But first, another small matter was nudging at Neverdie's mind. Long ago he had trapped an old enemy, Julian Ferrg, in his self-created prison. His conscience would not permit him to condemn that enemy to eternal living death. The world he would awaken to now would not be a pleasant one and it might kill him quickly, but Ferrg would have to take his chance on that.

Neverdie readied a small aircraft he also had stored in the vault and charged up its accumulator from the starship's power source. Then he opened the dome's launching hatch. Night had fallen, and starlight filtered through. With a sparkle from its rear the aircraft soared aloft and headed

North, passing over the wolves' campfires. Neverdie imagined the scenes that would be taking place below, and reaffirmed his opinion that Earth was no longer an abode for him.

On reaching Julian's tomb Neverdie spent some time clearing away earth and vegetation, then he cut an opening as he had done long ago. Inside Julian still lay as he had on that other occasion, untouched by the passage of time. As he looked down on the parchment-white face Neverdie's mandibles spread in the equivalent of a sad smile. He felt no resentment against the man. Julian was a courageous mite who had managed to preserve his tiny life in an attempt to challenge the long-living Aldebaranian, but the balance of his disadvantage lay too heavily against him. As for his viciousness and his greed, Neverdie hardly thought about that.

Finding the reviving mechanism serviceable, Neverdie set the timer for a few hours hence and then flew back to his starship. The charting of a course took slightly longer than he had expected, and it was early morning by the time he aroused the star-drive from its long sleep. He took one last, nostalgic look at the planet that had harboured him for what was, to him, a brief spell, and then took off. As its propulsion unit took hold on the fabric of space the deteriorated structure groaned slightly in the ether eddies. Neverdie scanned his instruments, watching anxiously for any sign of malfunction.

Disaster struck when he was only a few hundred feet in the air. The ship was *too* old, despite all the work he had put into her. An ominous *snap* came from aft. Noxious vapours filled the cabin. The ship began to fall and Neverdie struggled desperately with the controls.

As luck would have it, Julian was already awake by the time Neverdie attempted to leave the planet.

The suspended animation system was so effective that in a remarkably short time he had made a full recovery. With the coming of consciousness he found that the lid of the cylinder where he had slept had opened automatically, and he was already breathing air.

His limbs were stiff at first, but he eased himself from the cylinder, his mind already racing ahead to the tasks to come. Then a quick inspection acquainted him with the unexpected state of the chamber: the hole cut neatly in the wall, the decay of some of his equipment that was not carbon-bonded into diamond-hardness, the automatic calendar, calibrated up to a thousand years, that had stopped. Lastly, what he saw through the hole in the wall: a view of trees and fresh grass sweeping downhill. The trees, and the nearby flowers, were of a type unfamiliar to him.

A howl of torment burst from Julian's lips. It was as easy to read as an open book: the alien had outwitted him—disconnected the reviver and left him to sleep for countless ages. By now he would already have left Earth, perhaps centuries ago.

The desolation and disappointment that overtook Julian Ferrg with that realisation were almost enough to destroy him. Only one thing saved him from permanent emotional damage. He stepped to the opening, finding that the vault was actually buried in the hillside, and looked out, sniffing the air and smelling unfamiliar scents. He glanced upwards and saw something descending through the air leaving a trail of smoke. As it headed for a crash-landing he recognised Neverdie's starship and everything changed for him in an instant. He paused only to mark the landing place of the ship, then snatched up weapons and instruments from their sealed caskets and set off in wild pursuit.

The crashed starship was about three miles from the vault. Julian arrived there to find that Neverdie had crawled out and lost consciousness. He lay on a bank of green-and-purple flowers.

Julian was adapting quickly to his situation. To his senses the ages he had lain in the time-vault took on the subjective value of a few minutes only, and he required no lengthy reorientation. He took out the anaesthetic spray in case Neverdie should awaken and prove troublesome; but its contents had either denatured or leaked away and no spray issued. Tossing it to one side, he considered the problem of transporting Neverdie to his time-vault and hit on the idea of making a sledge.

Taking out his knife he cut down some nearby saplings and after one or two false starts fashioned a rough vehicle that, he thought, would serve. Then he ventured inside the creaking starship to see what he could find.

Tumbled about the small cabin were a number of objects that were strange to him. He would come back for them later, he promised himself. Luck was once again with him, for there was also a kind of rope-like harness that would be ideal for lashing his prisoner to the improvised sledge, and Julian set to work again with gusto, heaving the alien on to the shafts he had bound together with long grass and securing him in place. Once or twice Neverdie nearly came round and his diaphragm buzzed weakly. Julian ignored him.

Strapped to the underneath of his carapace Neverdie had an instrument with a narrow foot-long barrel that looked as though it might be a weapon. Julian took it from him and examined it. Though it was not designed for the human hand, his thumb found a stud. He pointed the barrel at a tree and pressed the stud. A dull red beam the colour of glowing iron traversed the space between and the tree suddenly changed colour and collapsed into fragments.

He smiled and thrust the weapon into the belt of his utility garment along with the other guns he already carried.

Hauling the load along the rough turf to his time-vault soon had him sweating, but he kept at it. He calculated that he had less than a mile to go when he was interrupted, first by a loud rustling in a nearby clump of vegetation, and then by the appearance of two of the inheritors of the Earth.

In a way they were grotesquely manlike. They could walk almost as easily upright as they could on all fours. Their forepaws were adapted for grasping, the toes having developed into tough, stubby fingers. In one of those paws the leading wolf carried a stone axe.

Julian looked at them, stunned. In like manner they stared back at him. Then the leader crouched, snarled and came at him in a bounding run with the axe upraised. Frantically Julian dropped the staves of the sledge and clawed at the pistol he carried in his belt. Gleaming yellow eyes stabbed into his brain. Then Julian drew and fired.

The shot rang out loudly. The wolf hurtled to the ground and lay there panting, blood beginning to ooze from the wound. The second creature paused for a moment, then turned and fled with a loping gait.

Taking careful aim, Julian squeezed the trigger again. The round failed to fire. Cursing, he pulled out Neverdie's weapon and destroyed the fleeing animal with its red beam.

Experiment revealed that every other round in his gun was dead. He had unknowingly played a game of Russian Roulette in reverse, and had come up with the only bullet that could have saved him. Luck was indeed with him today. And with Neverdie's weapon he would have no trouble in defending himself—if its charge lasted long enough.

Keeping a wary look-out, he continued on his way. Already he had identified his attackers as being descended from some wolf-like ancestor, but he wasted no time in thinking out the implications of that. The task in hand required all his concentration.

He encountered no more wolves before reaching the time-vault. Once inside, he first attended to making himself secure, finding the piece of vault wall that Neverdie had excised and using it, together with a workbench, to close the opening up again. It wouldn't hold against a determined assault, but he still had the alien gun.

Then he carried Neverdie into the vault's second chamber and strapped him to the main worktable. That done, he took time to rest, during which Neverdie awoke.

He could see that the alien had recovered, though no word came from him. Instead, Neverdie seemed to be looking around him, as if assessing his position. Finally Julian got up and began to inspect his equipment. At last Neverdie addressed a question, his voice slightly ragged through the diaphragm.

'I suppose it is no good trying to dissuade you?'

'Absolutely no good.'

Privately Julian was worried. Much of his equipment was still in good order—that part of it made of non-decaying material, like the surgical instruments. But much of it was useless. He no longer had any reagents, for instance, and would be hard put to make any chemical investigations. Almost all the research he could do was surgical anatomy.

The depressing fear of failure began to overcome him once again, but he made an effort to pull himself together. Perhaps torture would be the most effective method, he told himself, of finding out what he wanted to know.

He walked over to Neverdie and began laying out instruments. 'I haven't any anaesthetic,' he said in an apologetic tone. 'Unfortunately your species has a rather high nervous sensitivity, hasn't it? Make it easy on yourself, Neverdie. Co-operate and it will be quicker and less painful.'

As he spoke he wondered how much pain would induce *him* to give up an immortality he had already gained. Not any amount, in his opinion. Doubtless Neverdie was similarly motivated.

Nevertheless he got to work on the alien, who was strapped upside down like a huge overturned beetle. Some of his manipulations were torture, pure and simple, but some of them were a survey of Neverdie's anatomical and nervous systems. Neverdie gave vent to recurrent strangled shrieks and squirmed a good deal as far as his bonds would allow; but that was all. Julian remained aware of the need not to kill his subject and proceeded with care, but he did not feel over-anxious on that score. An immortal being must be physically capable of surviving quite drastic bodily disorder, he reasoned. After a while he absent-mindedly left off torture for its own sake and gave himself up to the enjoyment of study.

Nestling just below the brain was a spherical object, like a pearl two inches in diameter.

A massive nerve ganglion surrounded the shining ball, but no nerves, either axons or dendrites, appeared to be actually attached to it. The arrangement was like a nest containing a beautiful, perfect egg. To Julian's mind the sphere was an artificial object, not native to Neverdie's body, and he spent some time examining it.

'What will happen if I remove that pearly sphere just below your brain?' he asked, making sure that the alien was conscious.

There was no answer, so Julian, slowly and cautiously, did as he had threatened. He held the pearl up to the light in a pair of calipers and stared at it in fascination. He felt entranced, attracted, drawn on. The sphere seemed to radiate something into his mind, like a candle in otherwise absolute darkness.

A shuddering sigh whispered from Neverdie's voice diaphragm. 'It's done, then,' he said slowly, as though through a mist of pain.

'Is this what I was seeking?' murmured Julian.

'The Seed ... The Seed of Evil.'

Julian placed the pearl on the palm of his hand. It felt smooth and cool.

'You have nothing to defend any longer,' he said. 'Why not explain it all? I would appreciate it.'

With great effort Neverdie replied. 'It was not myself I sought to protect, but *you*. Let me make one last effort to dissuade you. The Seed you hold in your hand is the means to immortality, as you call it. Properly speaking it is biological permanence. All that is necessary is for the Seed to enter your body. To swallow it will be enough, for it will migrate to the most appropriate place, whereupon it will undertake to readjust all the body's functions with such perfection that it achieves ... biological perpetual motion. All the processes which normally cause decay are rendered null and void. The Seed's properties are even more remarkable than that. It will repair the most appalling injuries to its host; even if the body is completely destroyed it will lie quiescent until coming in contact with biological material, even if only humus, when it will endeavour to reconstruct that body, and usually it will succeed. Thus it is almost impossible to die, impossible even to commit suicide. The only way the arrangement can end is for the Seed to be taken away and given to someone else, whereupon it will forsake the old body and serve the new, for it is able to adapt itself to any conceivable living form in the universe.'

'So far you are making a poor job of dissuasion,' Julian commented.

'What would make such a life unbearable?'

Julian thought for a moment. 'Fear of losing it?'

'No. Guilt. The guilt of having stolen it.'

Julian laughed humourlessly. 'Do I look like a person who feels guilt?'

'No, but you will change. All change who receive the Seed. Everything looks different after a few million years—even after a few thousand. Yes, perhaps even after a few hundred years you will be tortured by the guilt which you must endure forever—or until——'

Neverdie's speech was interrupted by hoarse sounds of agony.

'It would be interesting to know how this remarkable device was manufactured,' Julian mused, unmoved by Neverdie's pain.

The alien seemed to recover enough to resume his explanations. 'I will tell you what I know. The origin of the Seed is lost in history, but the legend is plausible. It was created by a race of beings whose name I do not even know, and its purpose was *the punishment of a criminal*.'

Julian's attention was diverted by a sound of scratching on the wall of the vault. He hurried to the breach that Neverdie had made, put his ear to it and heard scufflings. Wolves? Or just an animal?

Picking up the death-beamer, he returned to Neverdie. His last remark had puzzled him. 'Continue!' he said sharply.

'My strength is failing,' said Neverdie. 'Nevertheless—these beings of whom I speak were faced with the problem of dealing with the greatest criminal of their experience, an individual who wilfully committed unspeakably foul acts, and who was without conscience. They decided that the most fitting punishment was first to reform him, and then to cause him to feel ceaseless remorse for his crimes. Immortality achieved both of these aims. And worse. For the other aspect of the life upon which you are so eager to embark is that you are doomed to be hunted by others who desire the immortality which only you possess. Thus those who made the Seed set in motion the chain of events of which you and I are a part. Wherever it goes the Seed attracts to itself the most evil of beings—no one knows how many have fallen into the same trap! The ceaseless hunt to steal immortality!'

'Anything worth having is worth fighting for,' Julian said. 'As for this remorse you find so terrible, I feel fairly immune from it.'

'*Now* you are—— You will change. I have not told you the worst. The worst is that eventually your very existence drags some other unfortunate into committing the same crime, suffering the same punishment—as I did to you. I was not always the harmless creature you know now, Ferrg. Oh, if you only knew—I was a hundred times worse than you! I stole the Seed, as you are stealing it. And I suffer, as you will suffer. I beg you, *do not accept the Seed.* Die, Ferrg, it is better to *die*!'

Julian interpreted Neverdie's argument as a last-minute attempt to con him. Even his claims concerning the miraculous powers of the Seed could be lies. Perhaps the little sphere was a capsule of poison. Julian decided he would have to take a chance on that.

'After coming all this way?' he said. 'I'm not backing out now.'

The sphere looked too big to swallow, but experimentally he put it in his mouth. As soon as it touched his lips it seemed to come alive, to be electric. Almost of its own accord it slid easily down his throat and he felt it in his stomach like a big, heavy globe which was slowly absorbed.

A heavy pounding rang all through him, as though he were full of vast cavities.

He seemed to lose touch with his surroundings, to be drawn into something vast and incomprehensible. He seemed to be hanging in an endless void, and suddenly all the people he had ever known flashed before his consciousness in quick succession. There was a lingering image of Ursula Gail as he had last seen her over a glass of wine, her bright hazel eyes regarding him sadly. He saw that all these people had vanished long ago into the void of non-existence, and inexplicably he envied them. Then the scene widened still further and he realised that he was being vouchsafed a vision. He saw that the sequence of events of which he was a part had begun long before the creation of the Seed. Long, long, long back in the vistas of time there had lived a race who had also succeeded in creating an immortal—a *true* immortal, much more so than any who came in possession of the Seed, which in the course of billions of years would itself perish. They had done it by printing an artificial consciousness into the fabric of space, and it could never be eradicated.

That consciousness was calling him. Its call had caused the Seed to be made in the first place. Somehow, sometime, one of the beings enchained by the Seed would, in due course, be lifted out of the material realm to share *Aeternus*' state, life without any of the means of life, and without end.

Aeternus' voice came to Julian: *You are my only-begotten son, with whom I am well-pleased.* And at that blasphemy he experienced a great fear that he was to be that eternal companion.

Suddenly it was over like a brief nightmare and he was standing beside Neverdie. The alien was speaking, his voice growing weaker.

'Hear them, Ferrg? Hear the Wolves? Do not fear—you

will get on well with them. You will be a leader. I remember when I first saw you that I recognised the wolf in you. Welcome to your *own* people—and thank you for releasing me. If you are lucky one of them might get you soon. However, the Seed will force you to put up a fight. That also is one of its functions——'

Julian said hastily: 'What can I do to give the Seed away?' But Neverdie did not answer, and he realised that the Aldebaranian was, at last, dead.

Outside, the wolves began to howl.